POKÉMON™

BLACK AND WHITE

VOL.15

Story by **HIDENORI KUSAKA**
Art by **SATOSHI YAMAMOTO**

**Pokémon Black and White
Volume 15
Perfect Square Edition**

**Story by HIDENORI KUSAKA
Art by SATOSHI YAMAMOTO**

© 2014 Pokémon.
© 1995–2014 Nintendo/Creatures Inc./GAME FREAK inc.
TM, ®, and character names are trademarks of Nintendo.
POCKET MONSTERS SPECIAL (Magazine Edition)
by Hidenori KUSAKA, Satoshi YAMAMOTO
© 1997 Hidenori KUSAKA and Satoshi YAMAMOTO/SHOGAKUKAN
All rights reserved.
Original Japanese edition "POCKET MONSTERS SPECIAL" published by SHOGAKUKAN Inc.
English translation rights in the United States of America, Canada, the United Kingdom,
Ireland, Australia and New Zealand arranged with SHOGAKUKAN.

English Adaptation / Bryant Turnage
Translation / Tetsuichiro Miyaki
Touch-up & Lettering / Susan Daigle-Leach
Cover Art Assistance / Miguel Riebman
Design / Fawn Lau
Editor / Annette Roman

Printed in the U.S.A.

Published by VIZ Media, LLC
P.O. Box 77010
San Francisco, CA 94107

10 9 8 7 6 5 4 3 2
First printing, April 2014
Second printing, May 2015

PARENTAL ADVISORY
POKÉMON ADVENTURES
is rated A and is suitable
for readers of all ages.
ratings.viz.com

www.perfectsquare.com

www.viz.com

Pokémon

BLACK AND WHITE

VOL.15

THE STORY THUS FAR!

Pokémon Trainer Black is exploring the mysterious Unova region with his brand-new Pokédex. Pokémon Trainer White runs a thriving talent agency for performing Pokémon. While traveling together, their paths cross with Team Plasma, a nefarious group that advocates releasing your Pokémon into the wild! Now Black and White are off on their own separate journeys of discovery...

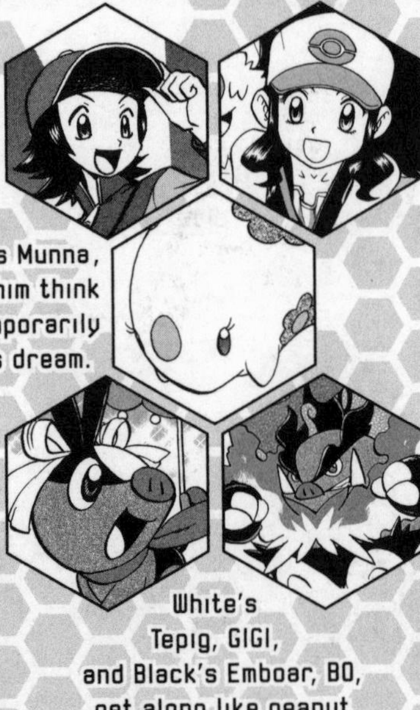

BLACK'S dream is to win the Pokémon League!

WHITE'S dream is to work in show biz... and now she's learning how to Pokémon Battle as well!

Black's Munna, MUSHA, helps him think clearly by temporarily "eating" his dream.

White's Tepig, GIGI, and Black's Emboar, BO, get along like peanut butter and jelly! But Gigi left White for another Trainer...Will White see Gigi again?

Adventure 49
A Misunderstanding

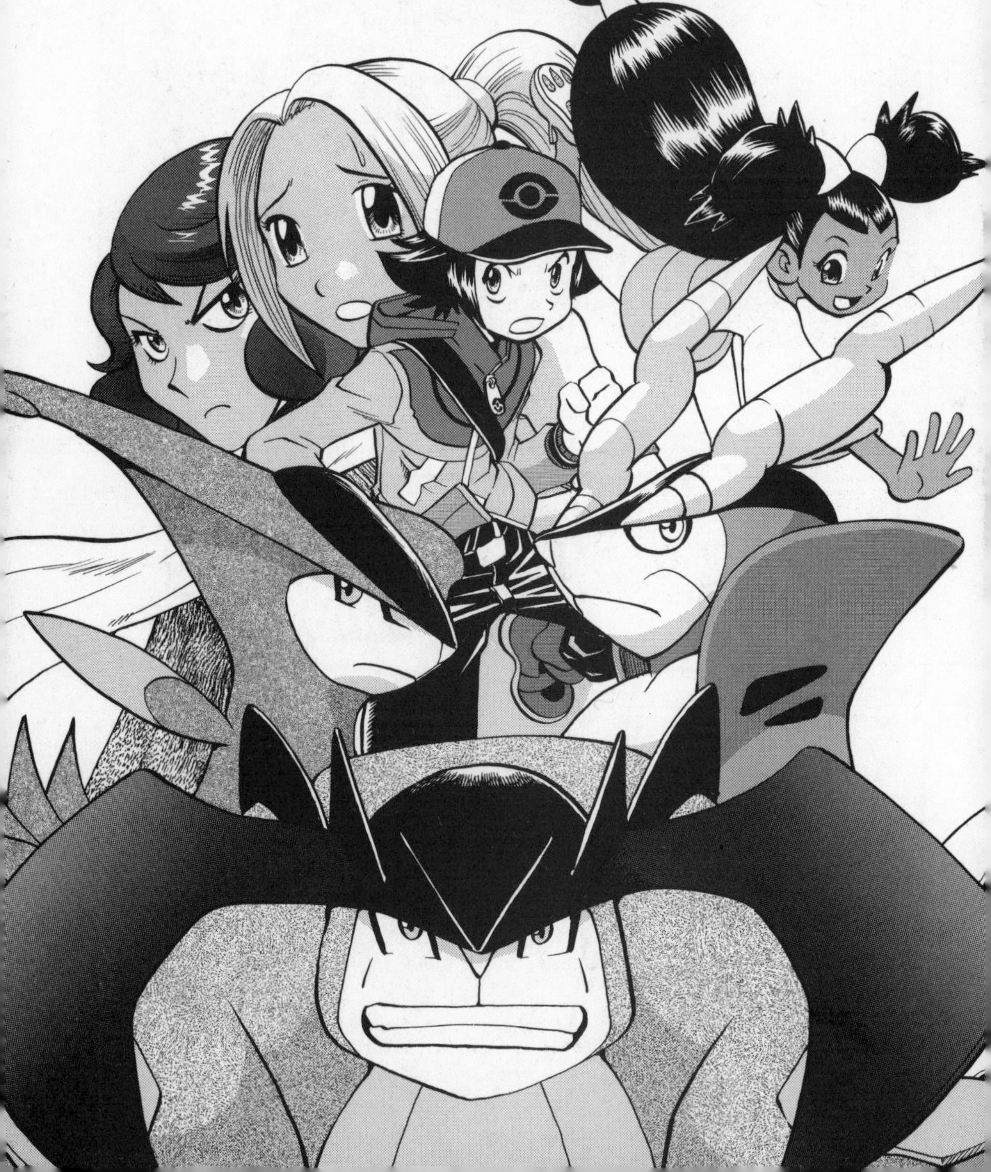

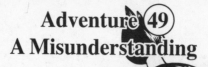

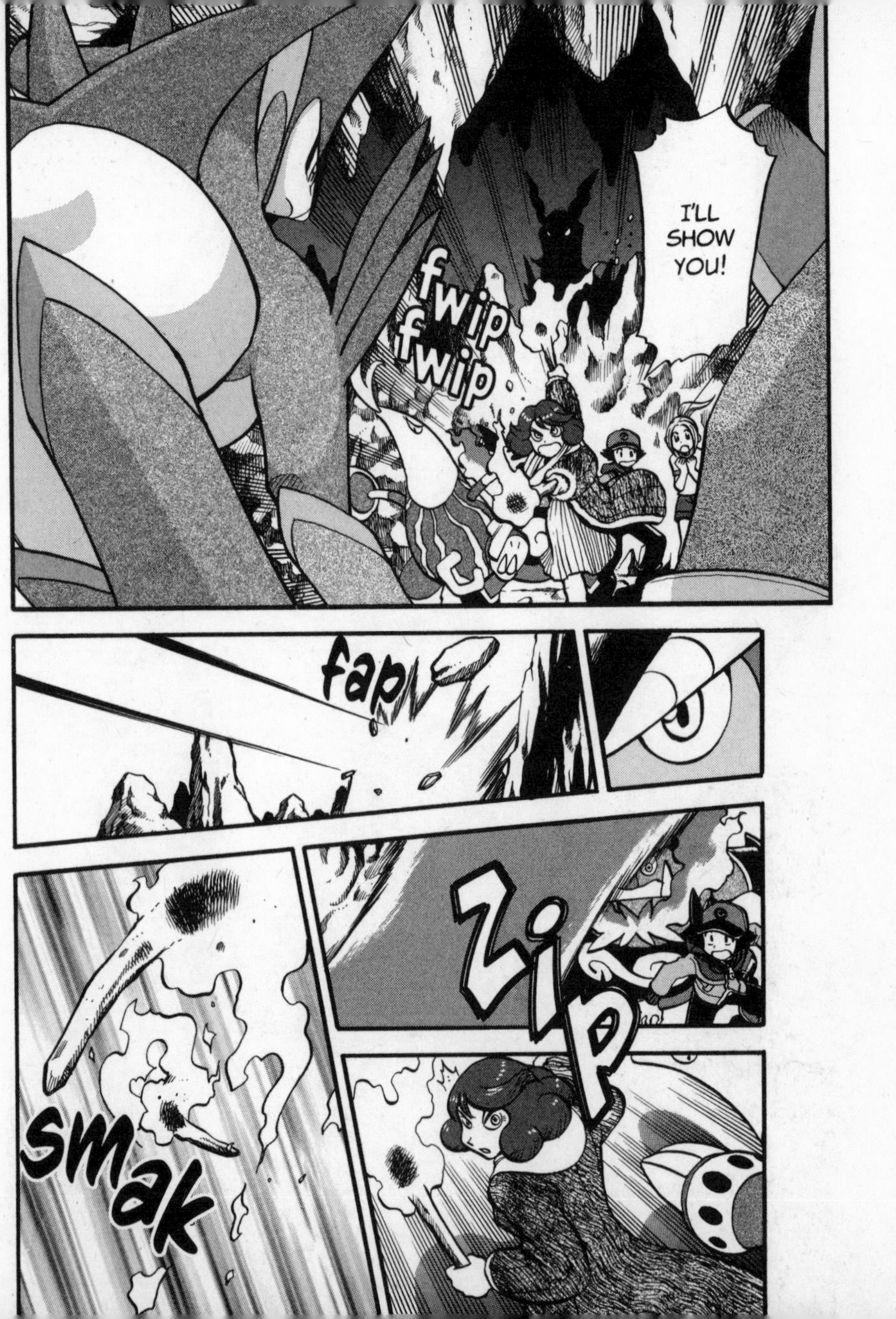
I'LL SHOW YOU!
fwip fwip
fap
Zip
smak

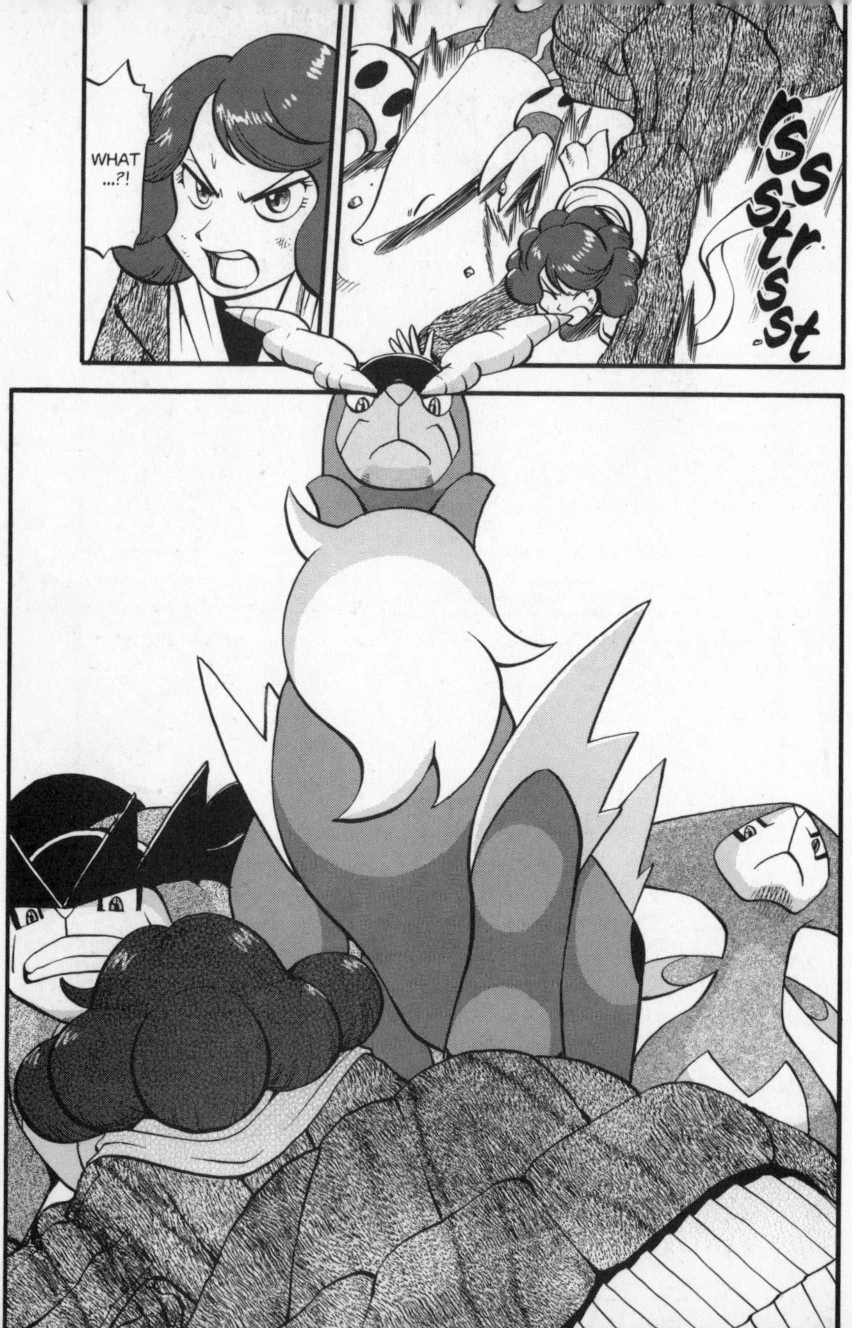
tssstrsst
WHAT ...?!

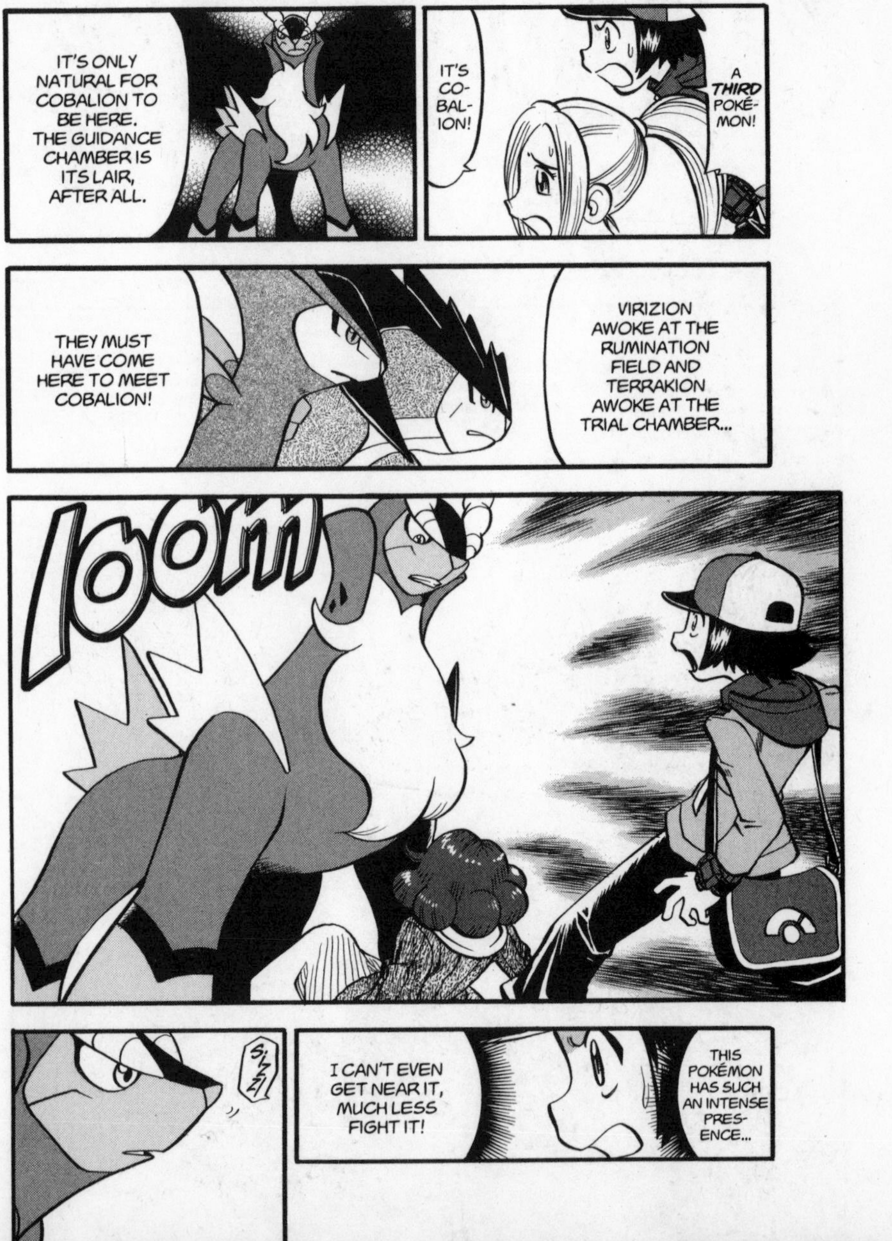
A THIRD POKÉMON!
IT'S CO-BAL-ION!
IT'S ONLY NATURAL FOR COBALION TO BE HERE. THE GUIDANCE CHAMBER IS ITS LAIR, AFTER ALL.
VIRIZION AWOKE AT THE RUMINATION FIELD AND TERRAKION AWOKE AT THE TRIAL CHAMBER...
THEY MUST HAVE COME HERE TO MEET COBALION!
IOOM
THIS POKÉMON HAS SUCH AN INTENSE PRES-ENCE...
I CAN'T EVEN GET NEAR IT, MUCH LESS FIGHT IT!
SIZZZ

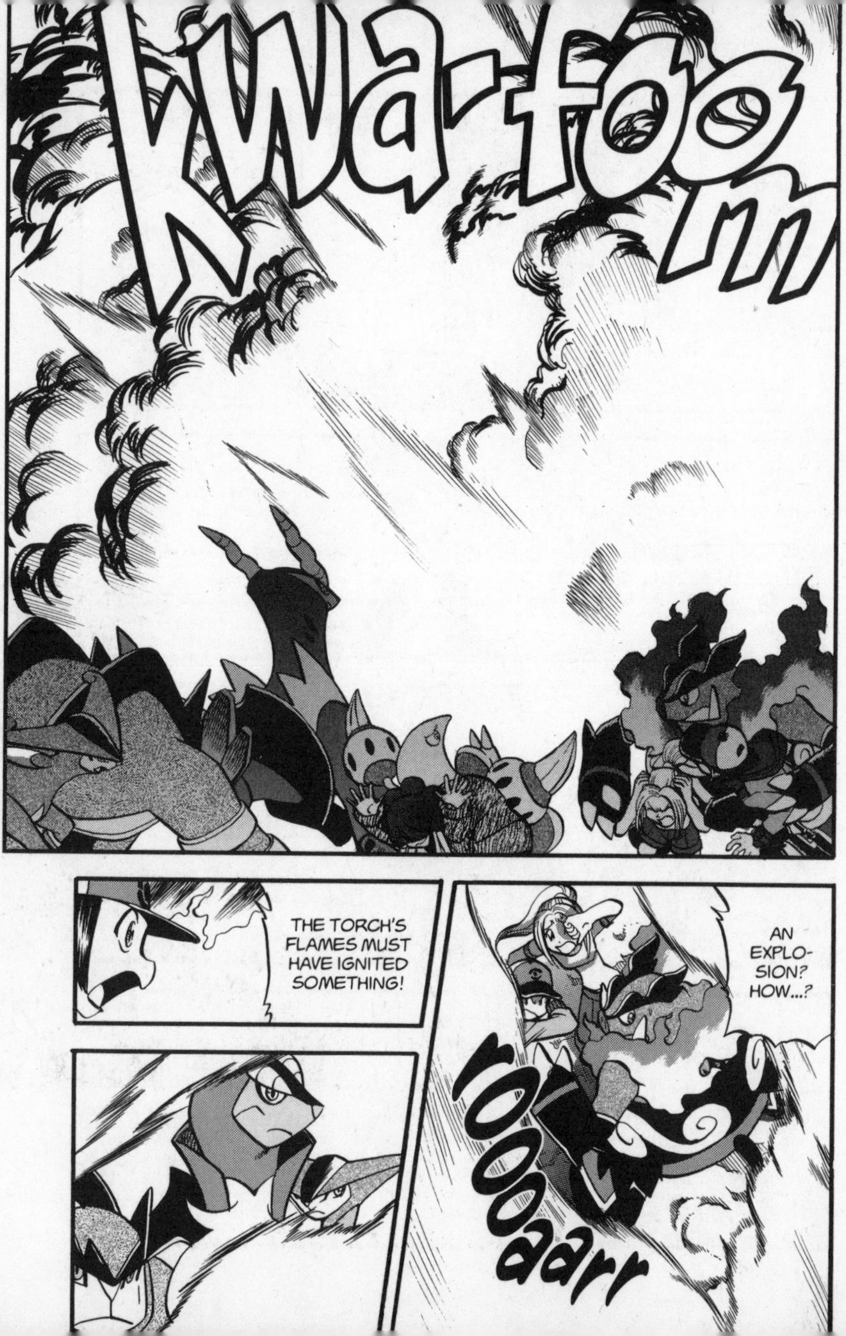
kwa-foom
AN EXPLO-SION? HOW...?
rooooaarr
THE TORCH'S FLAMES MUST HAVE IGNITED SOMETHING!

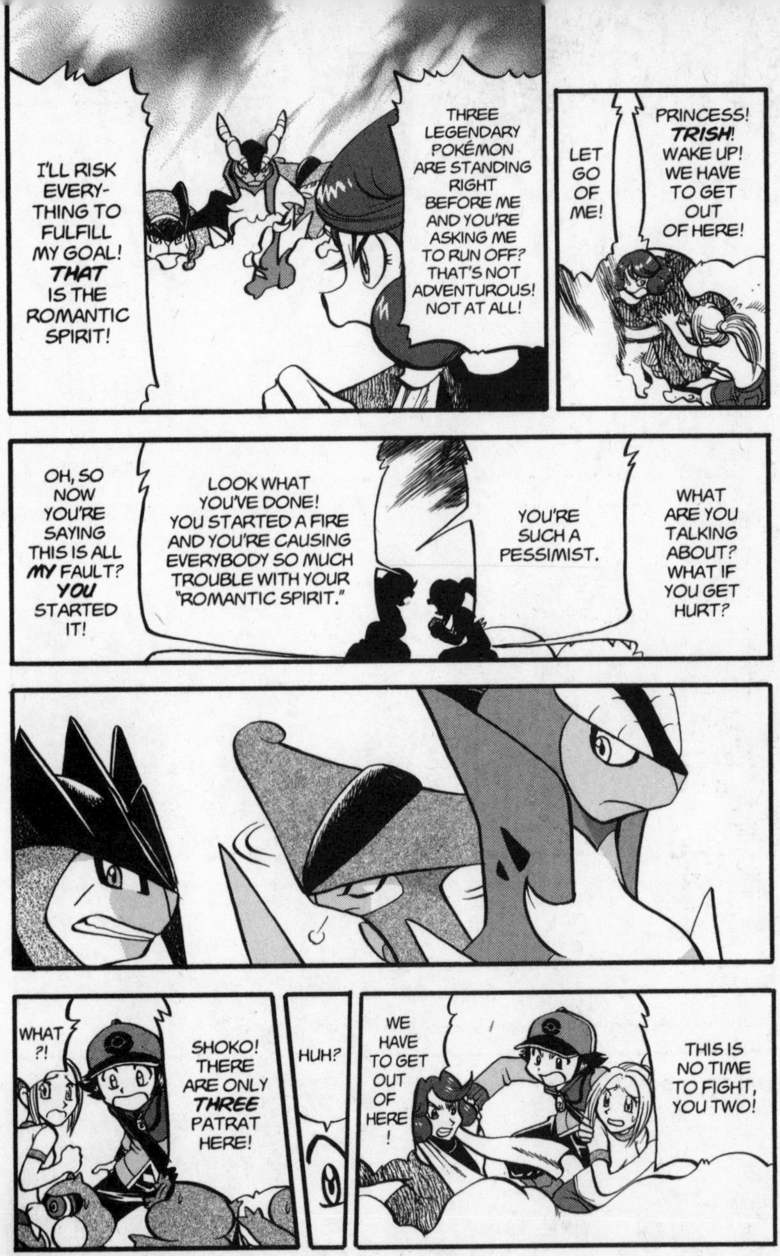
PRINCESS! TRISH! WAKE UP! WE HAVE TO GET OUT OF HERE!
LET GO OF ME!
THREE LEGENDARY POKÉMON ARE STANDING RIGHT BEFORE ME AND YOU'RE ASKING ME TO RUN OFF? THAT'S NOT ADVENTUROUS! NOT AT ALL!
I'LL RISK EVERY-THING TO FULFILL MY GOAL! THAT IS THE ROMANTIC SPIRIT!
WHAT ARE YOU TALKING ABOUT? WHAT IF YOU GET HURT?
YOU'RE SUCH A PESSIMIST.
LOOK WHAT YOU'VE DONE! YOU STARTED A FIRE AND YOU'RE CAUSING EVERYBODY SO MUCH TROUBLE WITH YOUR "ROMANTIC SPIRIT."
OH, SO NOW YOU'RE SAYING THIS IS ALL MY FAULT? YOU STARTED IT!
THIS IS NO TIME TO FIGHT, YOU TWO!
WE HAVE TO GET OUT OF HERE!
HUH?
SHOKO! THERE ARE ONLY THREE PATRAT HERE!
WHAT?!

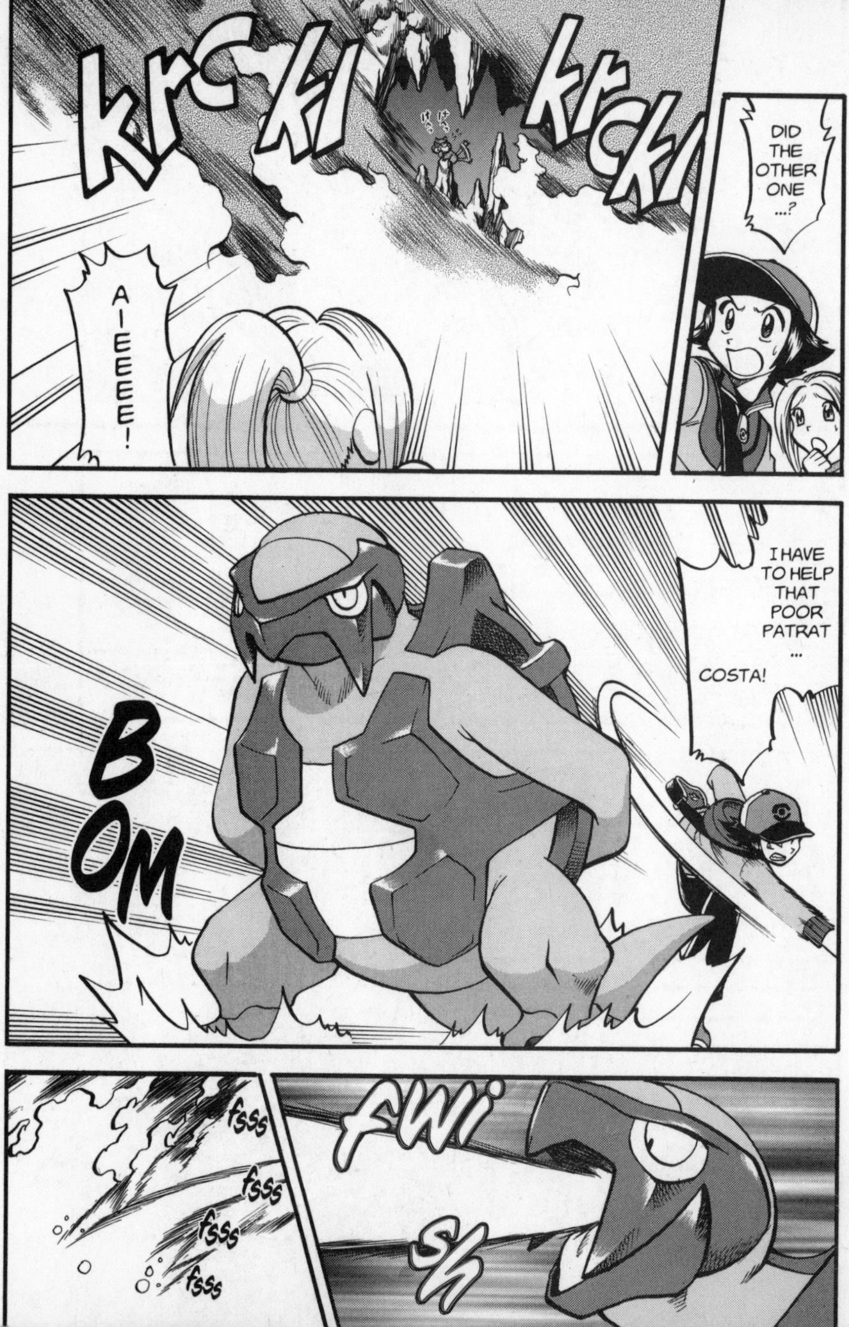
DID THE OTHER ONE ...?
krcki
krck!
AIEEEE!
I HAVE TO HELP THAT POOR PATRAT ...
COSTA!
BOOM
fwish
fsss
fsss
fsss
fsss

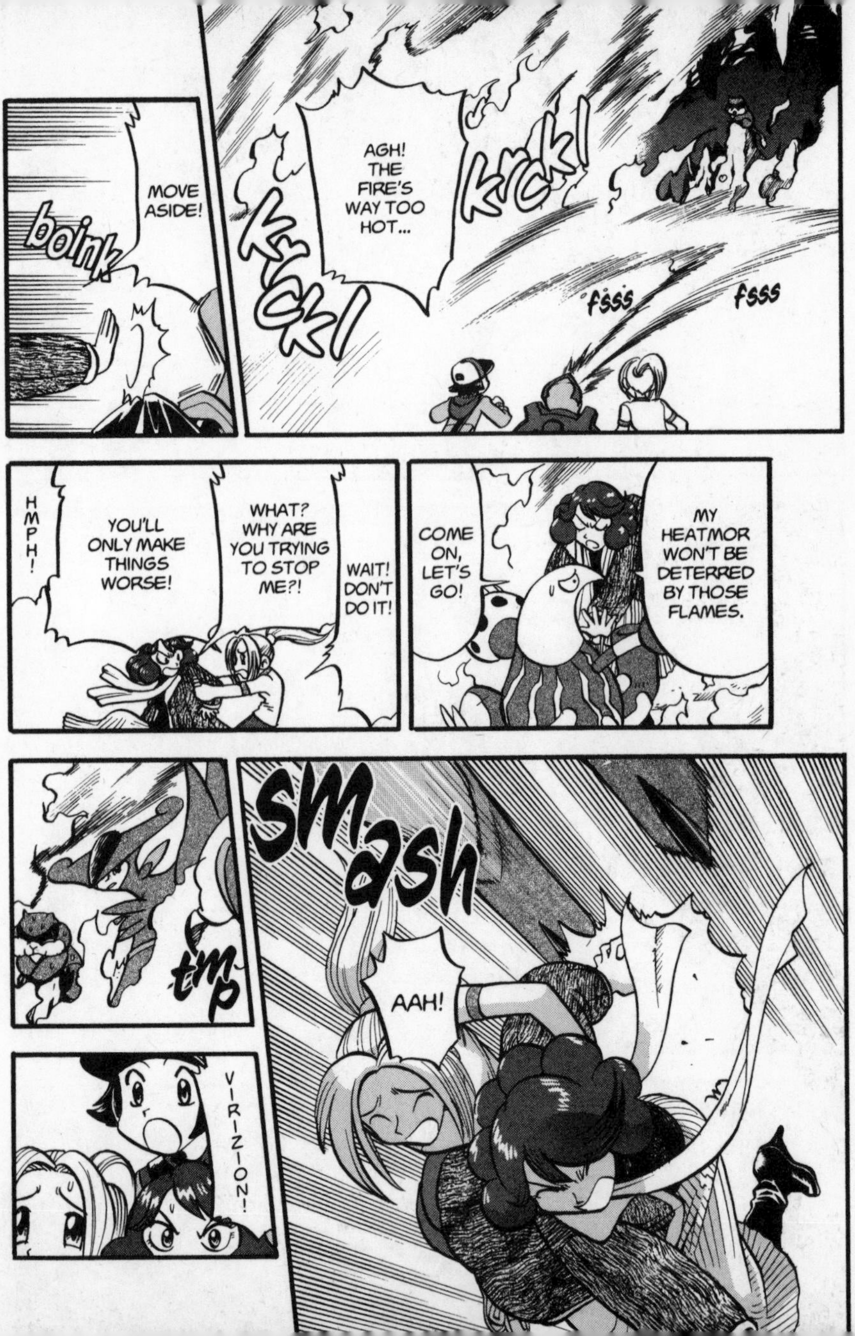

krckl
AGH! THE FIRE'S WAY TOO HOT...
krckl
fsss
fsss
MOVE ASIDE!
boink
MY HEATMOR WON'T BE DETERRED BY THOSE FLAMES.
COME ON, LET'S GO!
WAIT! DON'T DO IT!
WHAT? WHY ARE YOU TRYING TO STOP ME?!
YOU'LL ONLY MAKE THINGS WORSE!
HMPH!
smash
AAH!
tmp
VIRIZION!

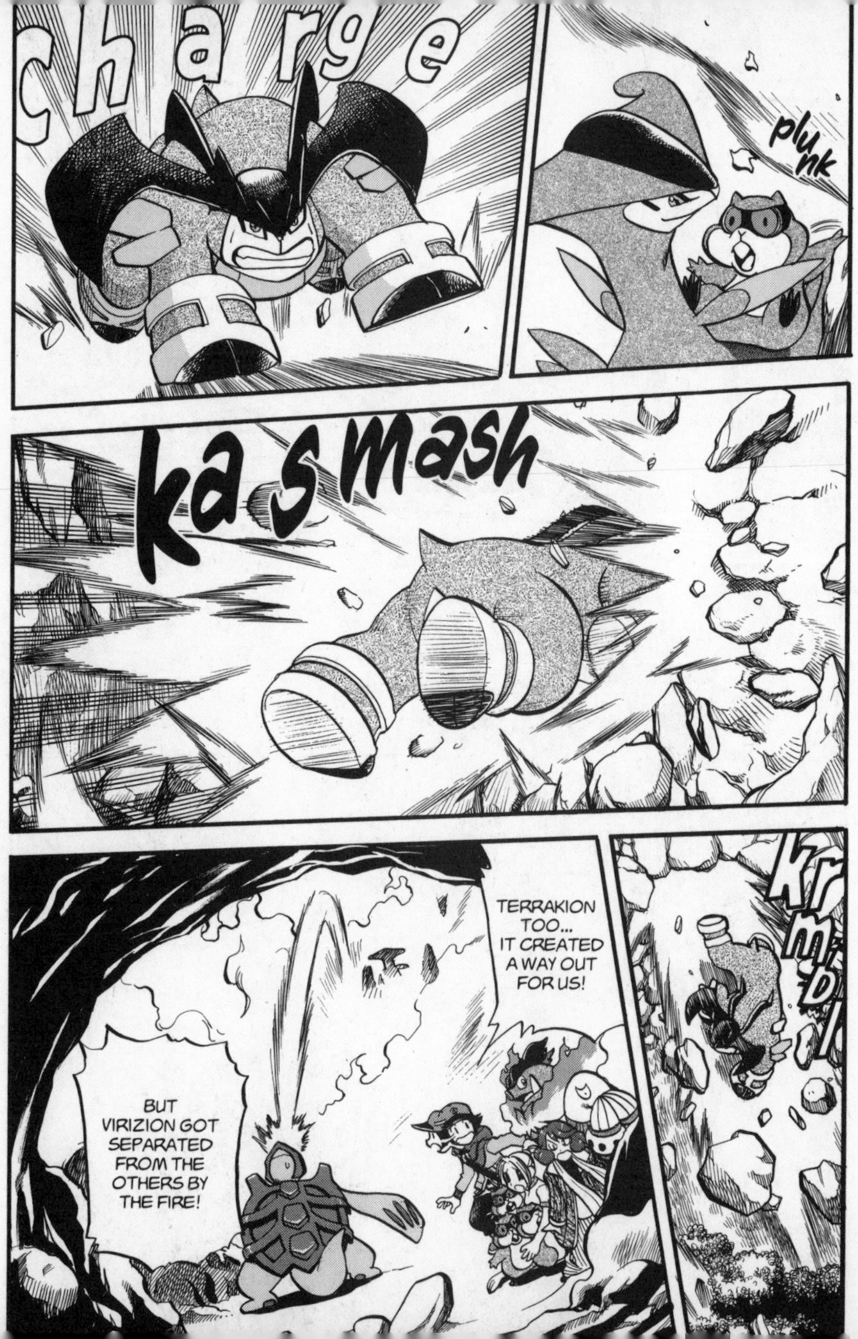

plunk
charge
ka smash
krmbl
TERRAKION TOO... IT CREATED A WAY OUT FOR US!
BUT VIRIZION GOT SEPARATED FROM THE OTHERS BY THE FIRE!

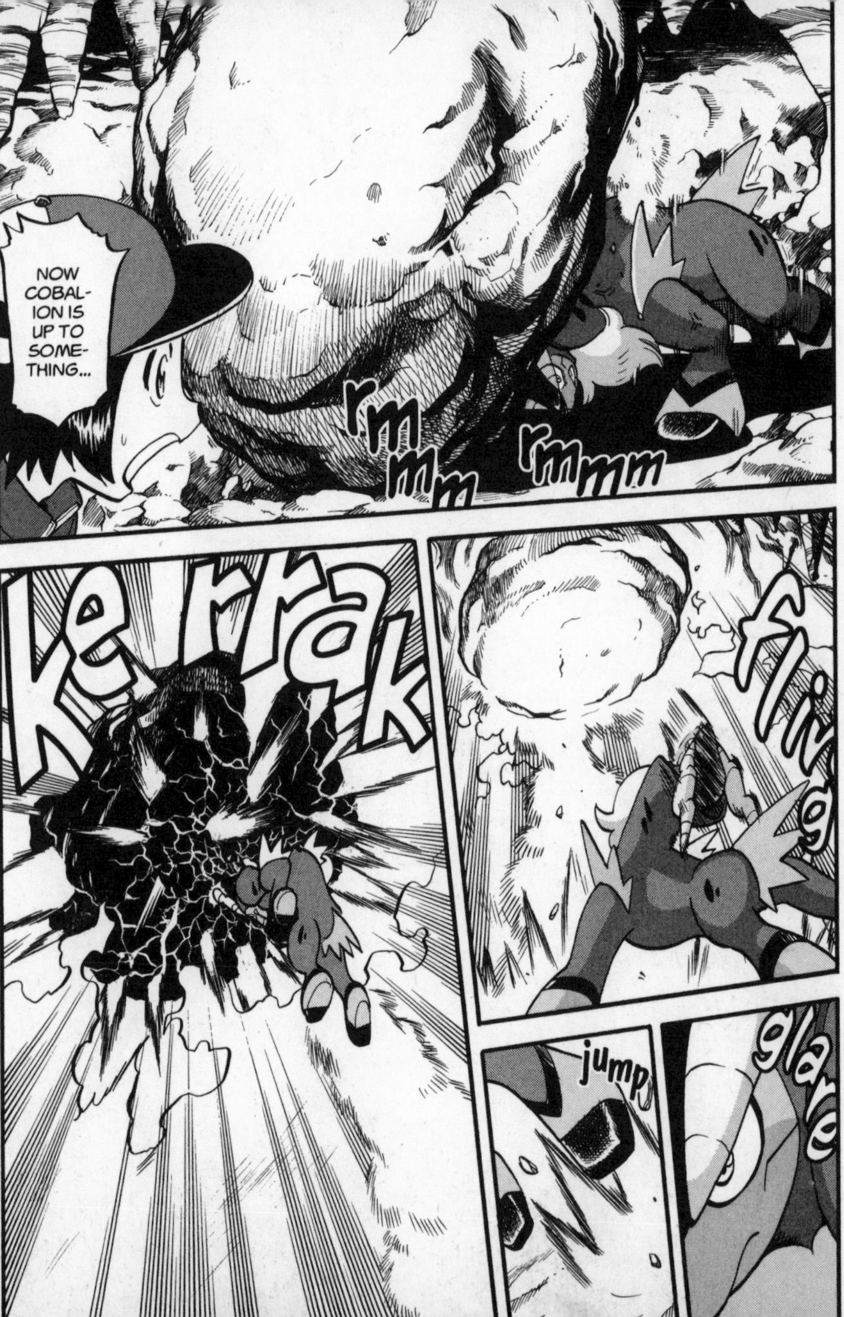
NOW COBALION IS UP TO SOMETHING...
rmmmm
rmmmm
fling
glare
jump
kerrak

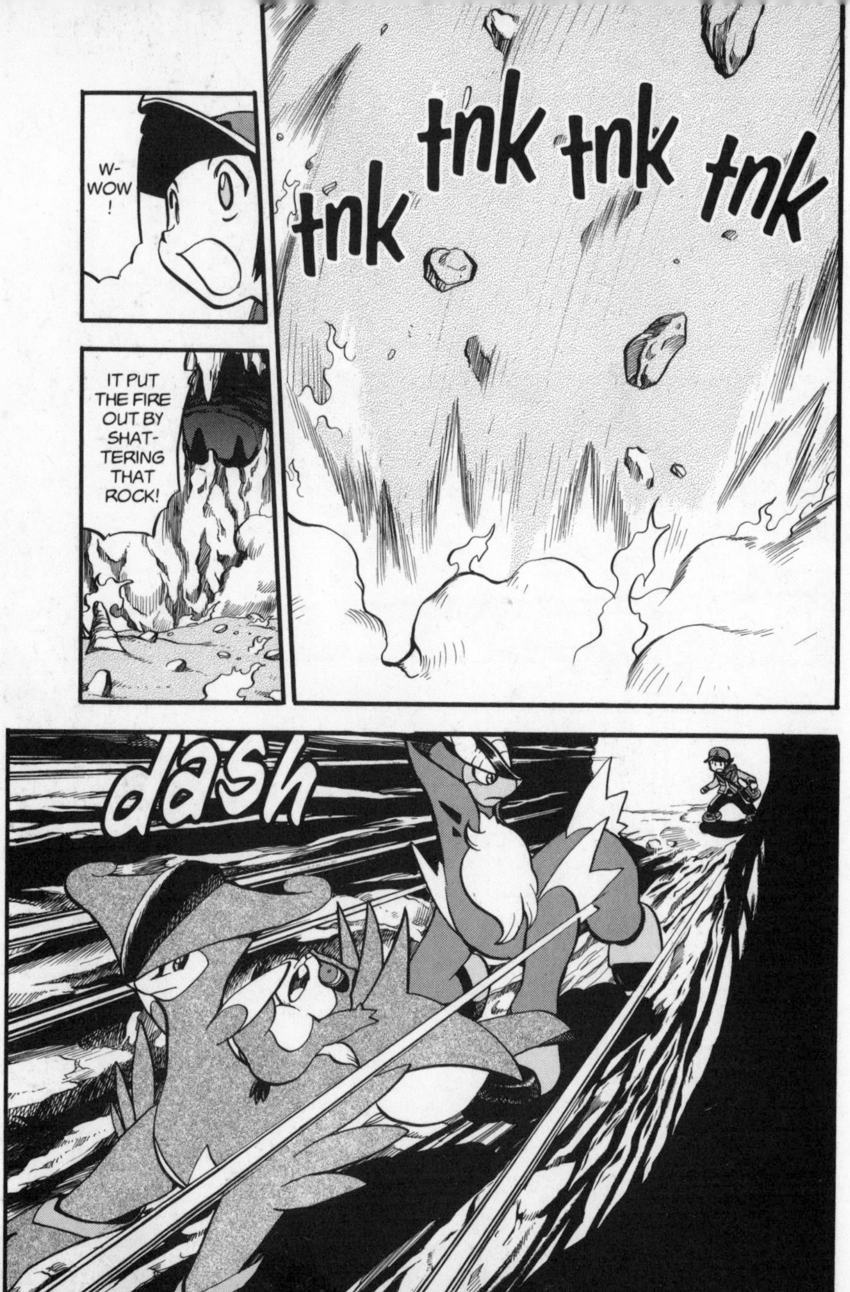
tnk tnk tnk tnk
W-WOW!
IT PUT THE FIRE OUT BY SHATTERING THAT ROCK!
dash

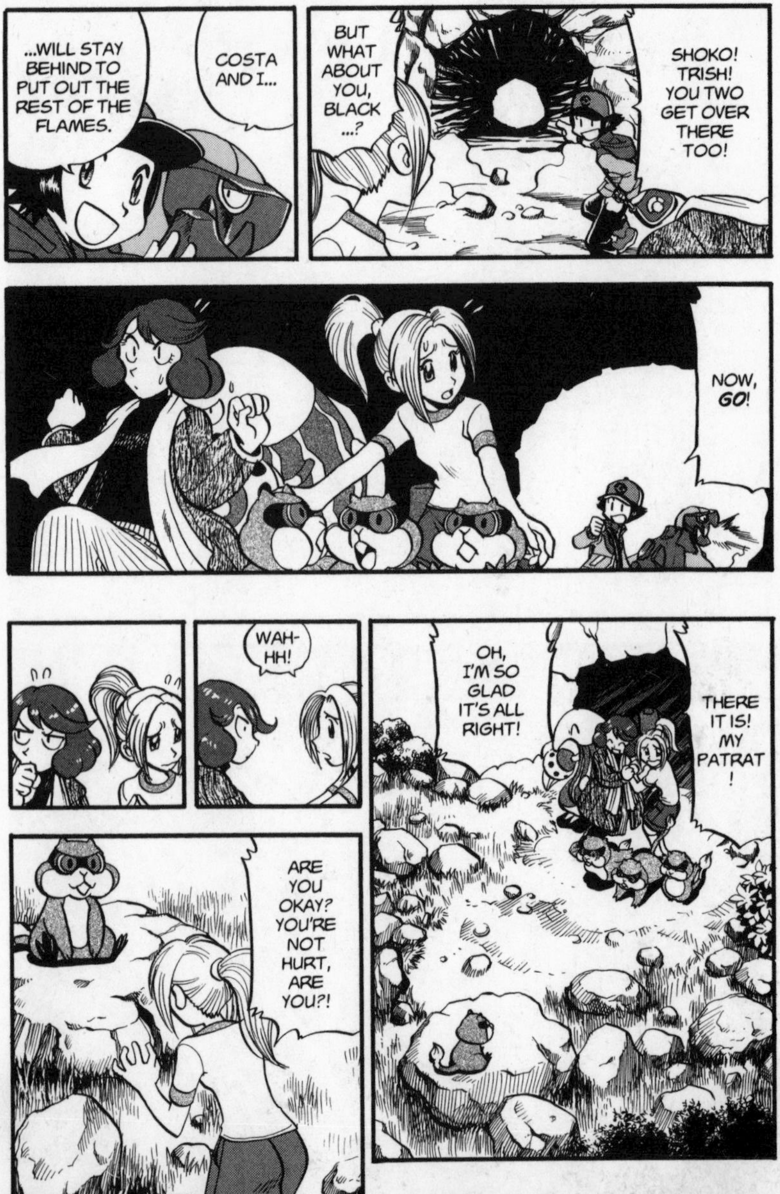
SHOKO! TRISH! YOU TWO GET OVER THERE TOO!
BUT WHAT ABOUT YOU, BLACK ...?
COSTA AND I...
...WILL STAY BEHIND TO PUT OUT THE REST OF THE FLAMES.
NOW, GO!
THERE IT IS! MY PATRAT !
OH, I'M SO GLAD IT'S ALL RIGHT!
WAH-HH!
ARE YOU OKAY? YOU'RE NOT HURT, ARE YOU?!

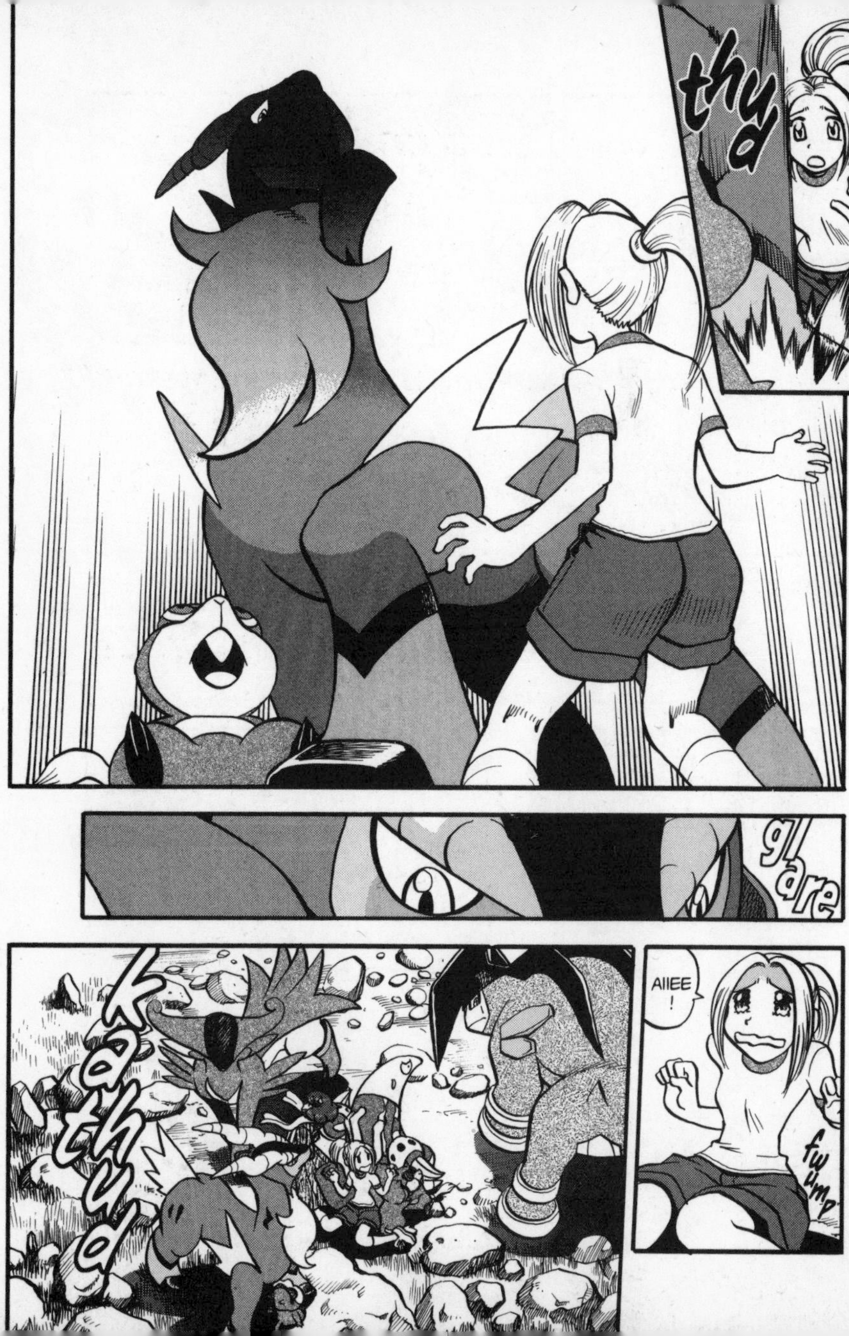
thud
glare
AIIEE!
fwump
kathud

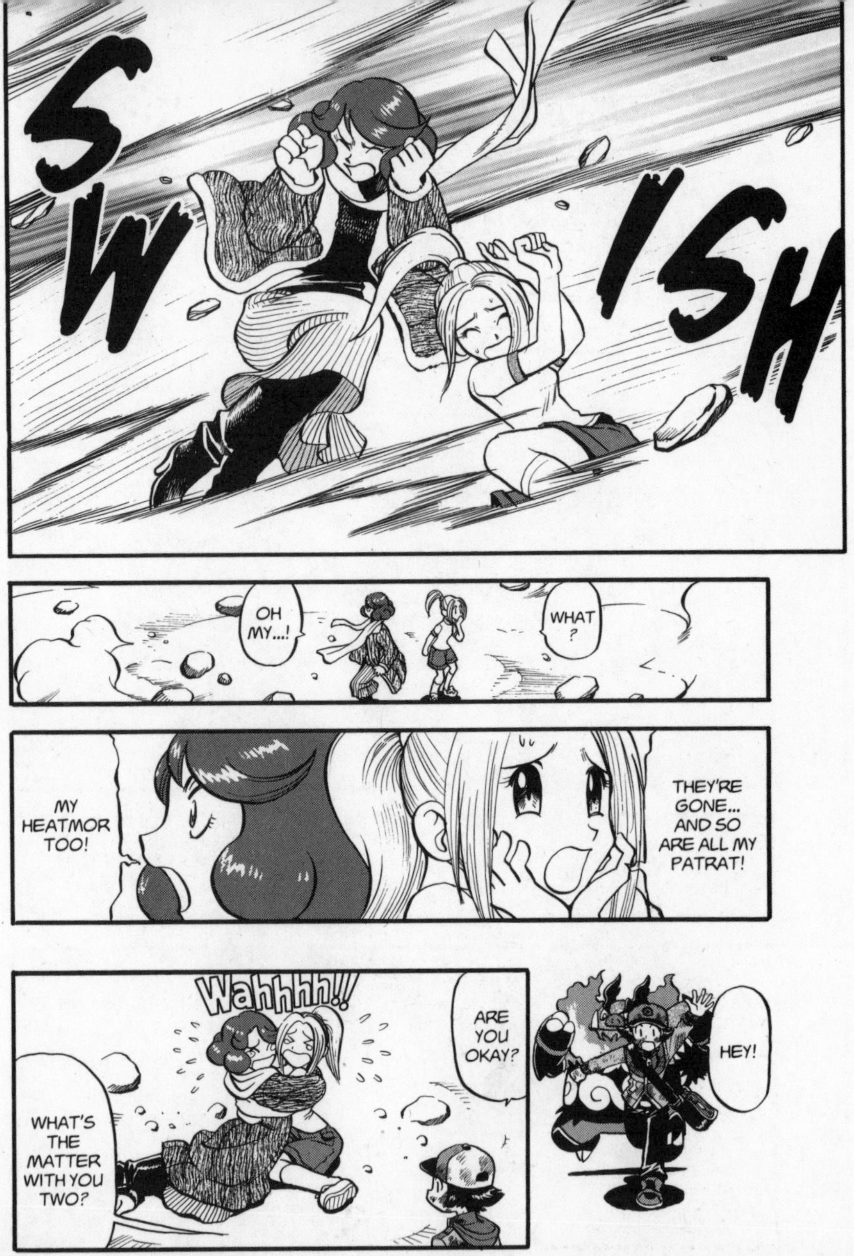
SWISH
WHAT ?
OH MY...!
THEY'RE GONE... AND SO ARE ALL MY PATRAT!
MY HEATMOR TOO!
HEY!
ARE YOU OKAY?
Wahhhh!!
WHAT'S THE MATTER WITH YOU TWO?

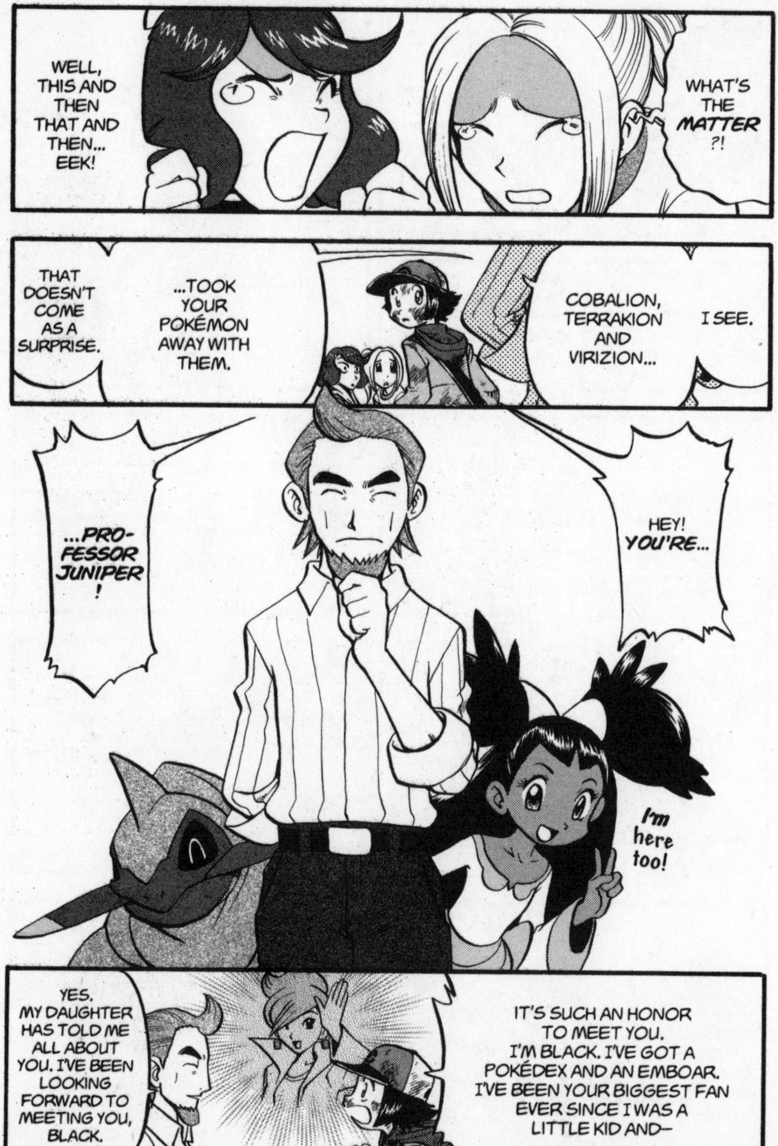
WHAT'S THE MATTER ?!
WELL, THIS AND THEN THAT AND THEN... EEK!
I SEE.
COBALION, TERRAKION AND VIRIZION...
...TOOK YOUR POKÉMON AWAY WITH THEM.
THAT DOESN'T COME AS A SURPRISE.
HEY! YOU'RE...
...PRO-FESSOR JUNIPER!
I'm here too!
IT'S SUCH AN HONOR TO MEET YOU. I'M BLACK. I'VE GOT A POKÉDEX AND AN EMBOAR. I'VE BEEN YOUR BIGGEST FAN EVER SINCE I WAS A LITTLE KID AND—
YES. MY DAUGHTER HAS TOLD ME ALL ABOUT YOU. I'VE BEEN LOOKING FORWARD TO MEETING YOU, BLACK.

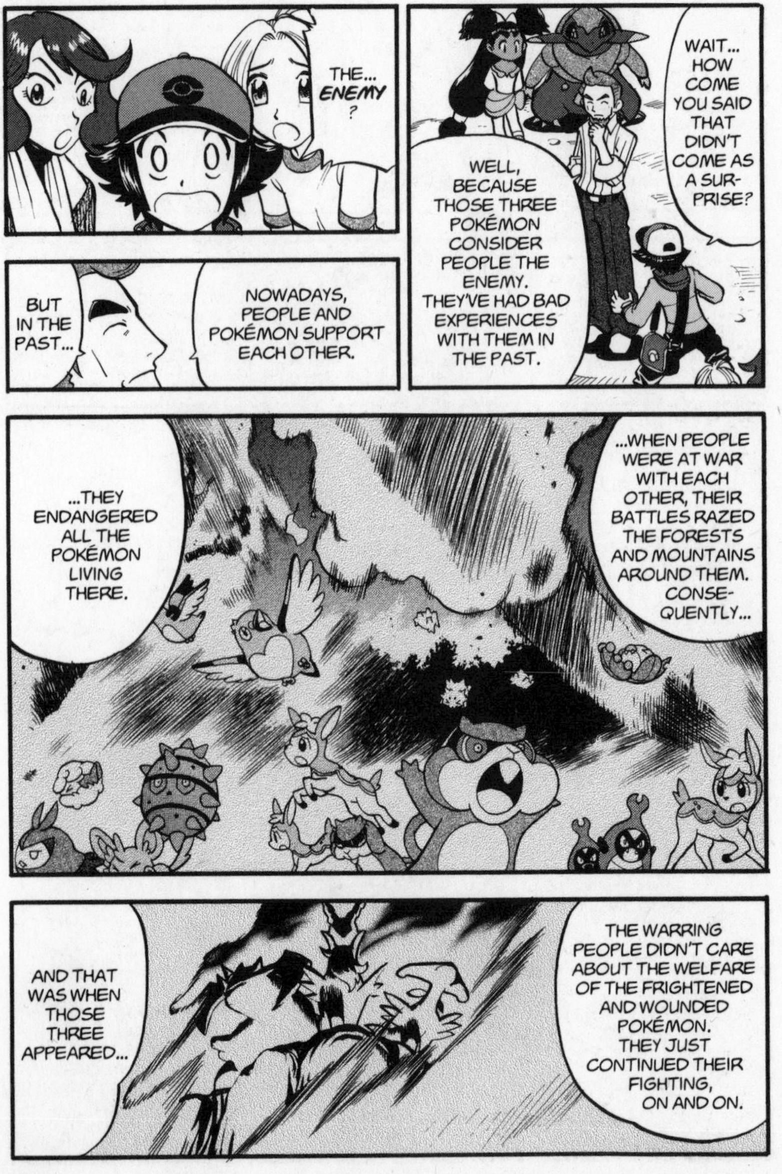
WAIT... HOW COME YOU SAID THAT DIDN'T COME AS A SUR-PRISE?
WELL, BECAUSE THOSE THREE POKÉMON CONSIDER PEOPLE THE ENEMY. THEY'VE HAD BAD EXPERIENCES WITH THEM IN THE PAST.
THE... *ENEMY* ?
NOWADAYS, PEOPLE AND POKÉMON SUPPORT EACH OTHER.
BUT IN THE PAST...
...WHEN PEOPLE WERE AT WAR WITH EACH OTHER, THEIR BATTLES RAZED THE FORESTS AND MOUNTAINS AROUND THEM. CONSE-QUENTLY...
...THEY ENDANGERED ALL THE POKÉMON LIVING THERE.
THE WARRING PEOPLE DIDN'T CARE ABOUT THE WELFARE OF THE FRIGHTENED AND WOUNDED POKÉMON. THEY JUST CONTINUED THEIR FIGHTING, ON AND ON.
AND THAT WAS WHEN THOSE THREE APPEARED...

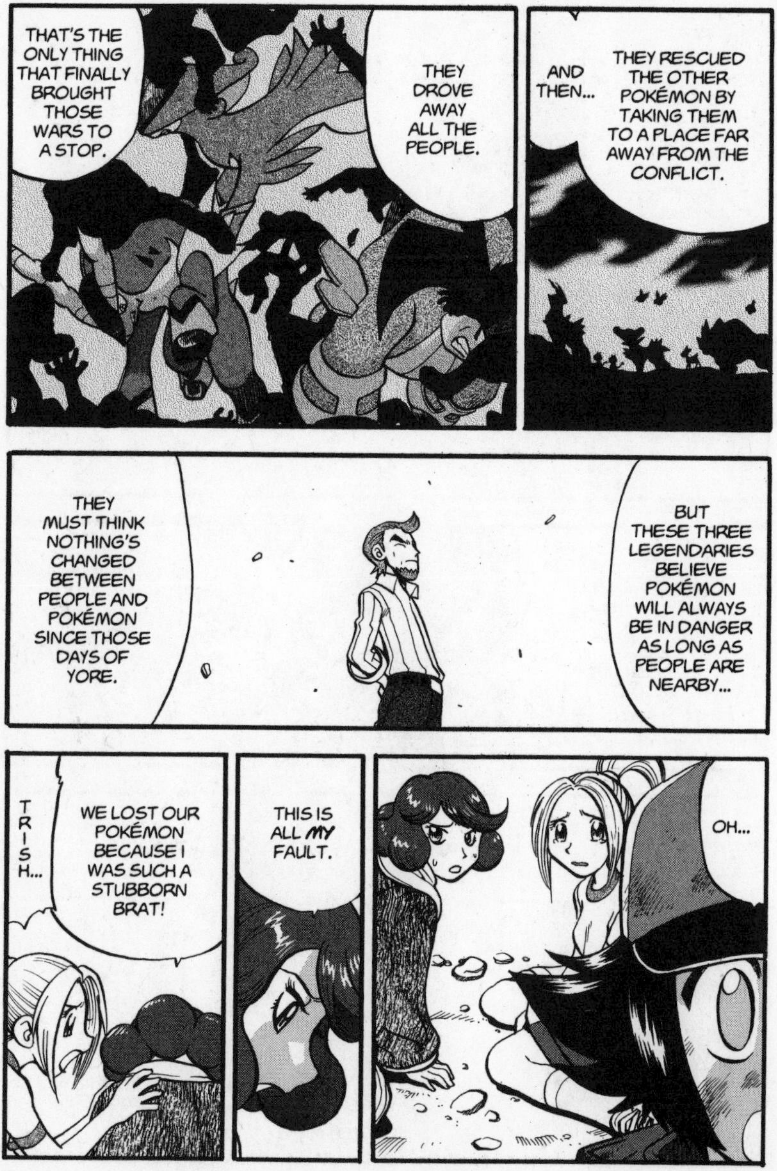
THAT'S THE ONLY THING THAT FINALLY BROUGHT THOSE WARS TO A STOP.
THEY DROVE AWAY ALL THE PEOPLE.
AND THEN...
THEY RESCUED THE OTHER POKÉMON BY TAKING THEM TO A PLACE FAR AWAY FROM THE CONFLICT.
THEY MUST THINK NOTHING'S CHANGED BETWEEN PEOPLE AND POKÉMON SINCE THOSE DAYS OF YORE.
BUT THESE THREE LEGENDARIES BELIEVE POKÉMON WILL ALWAYS BE IN DANGER AS LONG AS PEOPLE ARE NEARBY...
TRISH...
WE LOST OUR POKÉMON BECAUSE I WAS SUCH A STUBBORN BRAT!
THIS IS ALL *MY* FAULT.
OH...

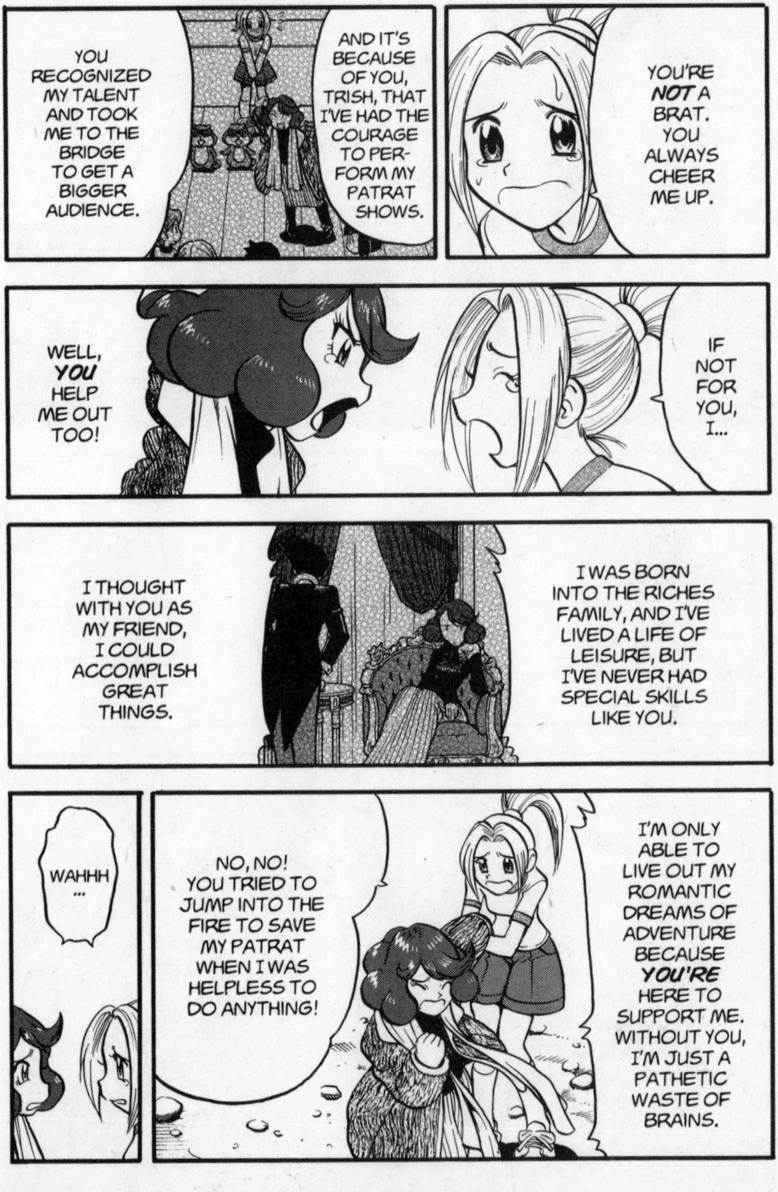
YOU'RE NOT A BRAT. YOU ALWAYS CHEER ME UP.
AND IT'S BECAUSE OF YOU, TRISH, THAT I'VE HAD THE COURAGE TO PER-FORM MY PATRAT SHOWS.
YOU RECOGNIZED MY TALENT AND TOOK ME TO THE BRIDGE TO GET A BIGGER AUDIENCE.
IF NOT FOR YOU, I...
WELL, YOU HELP ME OUT TOO!
I WAS BORN INTO THE RICHES FAMILY, AND I'VE LIVED A LIFE OF LEISURE, BUT I'VE NEVER HAD SPECIAL SKILLS LIKE YOU.
I THOUGHT WITH YOU AS MY FRIEND, I COULD ACCOMPLISH GREAT THINGS.
I'M ONLY ABLE TO LIVE OUT MY ROMANTIC DREAMS OF ADVENTURE BECAUSE YOU'RE HERE TO SUPPORT ME. WITHOUT YOU, I'M JUST A PATHETIC WASTE OF BRAINS.
NO, NO! YOU TRIED TO JUMP INTO THE FIRE TO SAVE MY PATRAT WHEN I WAS HELPLESS TO DO ANYTHING!
WAHHH ...

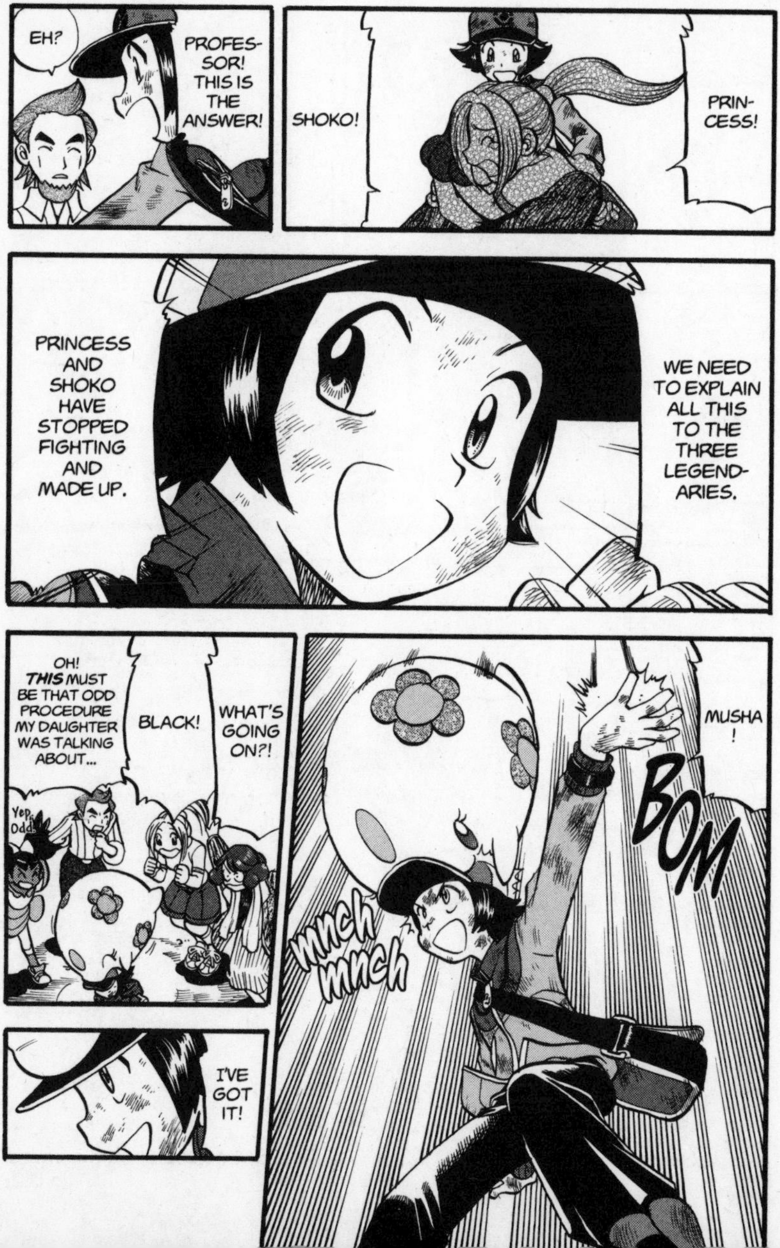
PRIN-
CESS!
SHOKO!
PROFES-
SOR!
THIS IS
THE
ANSWER!
EH?
WE NEED TO EXPLAIN ALL THIS TO THE THREE LEGEND-ARIES.
PRINCESS AND SHOKO HAVE STOPPED FIGHTING AND MADE UP.
MUSHA!
BOM
mnch mnch
WHAT'S GOING ON?!
BLACK!
OH! **THIS** MUST BE THAT ODD PROCEDURE MY DAUGHTER WAS TALKING ABOUT...
Yep. Odd.
I'VE GOT IT!

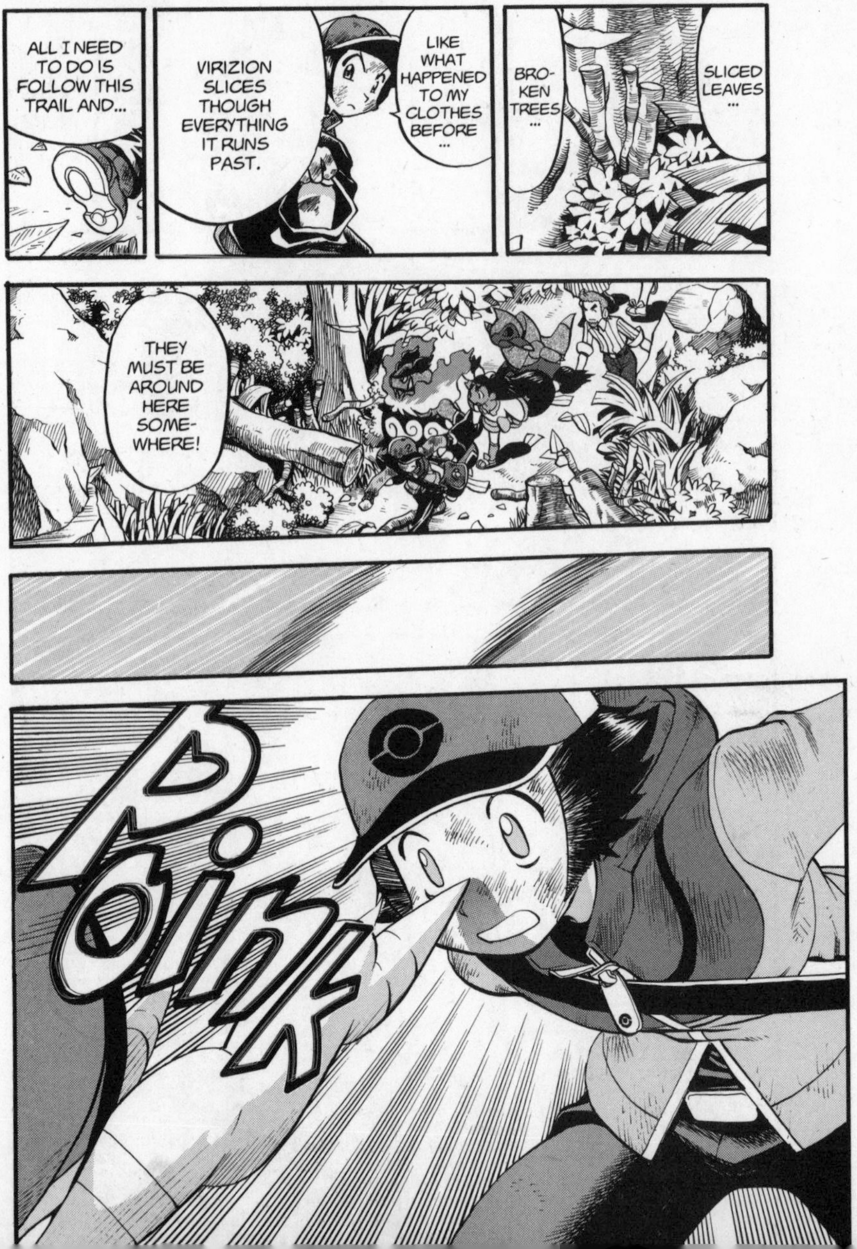
SLICED LEAVES ...
BRO-KEN TREES ...
LIKE WHAT HAPPENED TO MY CLOTHES BEFORE ...
VIRIZION SLICES THOUGH EVERYTHING IT RUNS PAST.
ALL I NEED TO DO IS FOLLOW THIS TRAIL AND...
THEY MUST BE AROUND HERE SOME-WHERE!
Poink

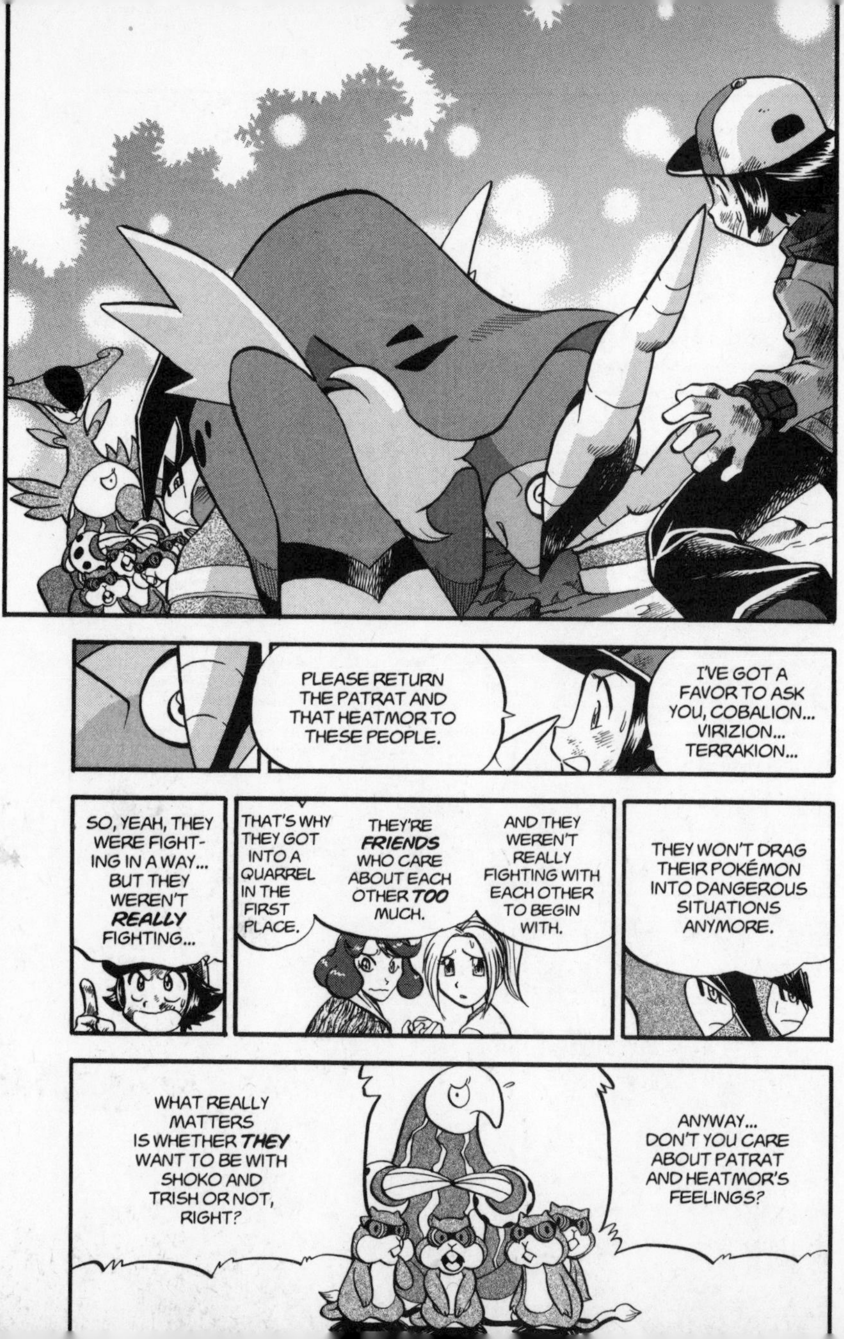

I'VE GOT A FAVOR TO ASK YOU, COBALION... VIRIZION... TERRAKION...
PLEASE RETURN THE PATRAT AND THAT HEATMOR TO THESE PEOPLE.
THEY WON'T DRAG THEIR POKÉMON INTO DANGEROUS SITUATIONS ANYMORE.
AND THEY WEREN'T REALLY FIGHTING WITH EACH OTHER TO BEGIN WITH.
THEY'RE ***FRIENDS*** WHO CARE ABOUT EACH OTHER ***TOO*** MUCH.
THAT'S WHY THEY GOT INTO A QUARREL IN THE FIRST PLACE.
SO, YEAH, THEY WERE FIGHTING IN A WAY... BUT THEY WEREN'T ***REALLY*** FIGHTING...
ANYWAY... DON'T YOU CARE ABOUT PATRAT AND HEATMOR'S FEELINGS?
WHAT REALLY MATTERS IS WHETHER ***THEY*** WANT TO BE WITH SHOKO AND TRISH OR NOT, RIGHT?

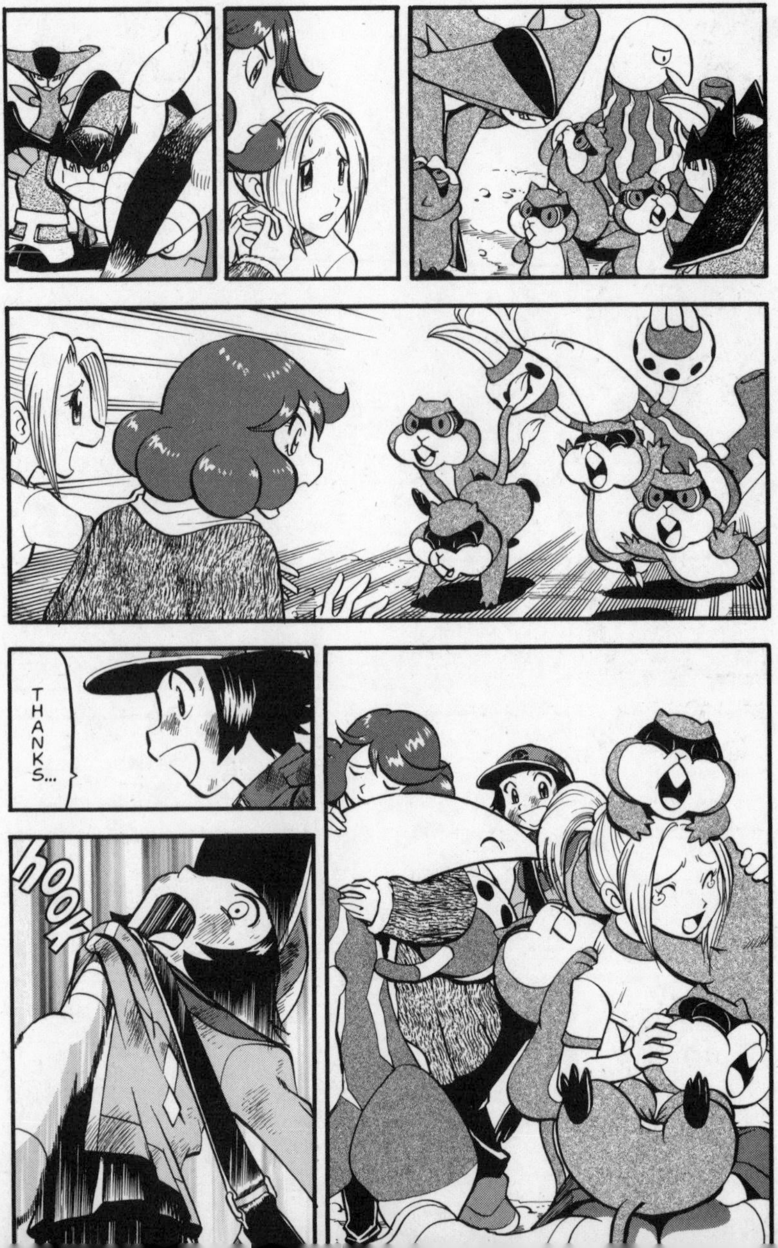
THANKS...
hook

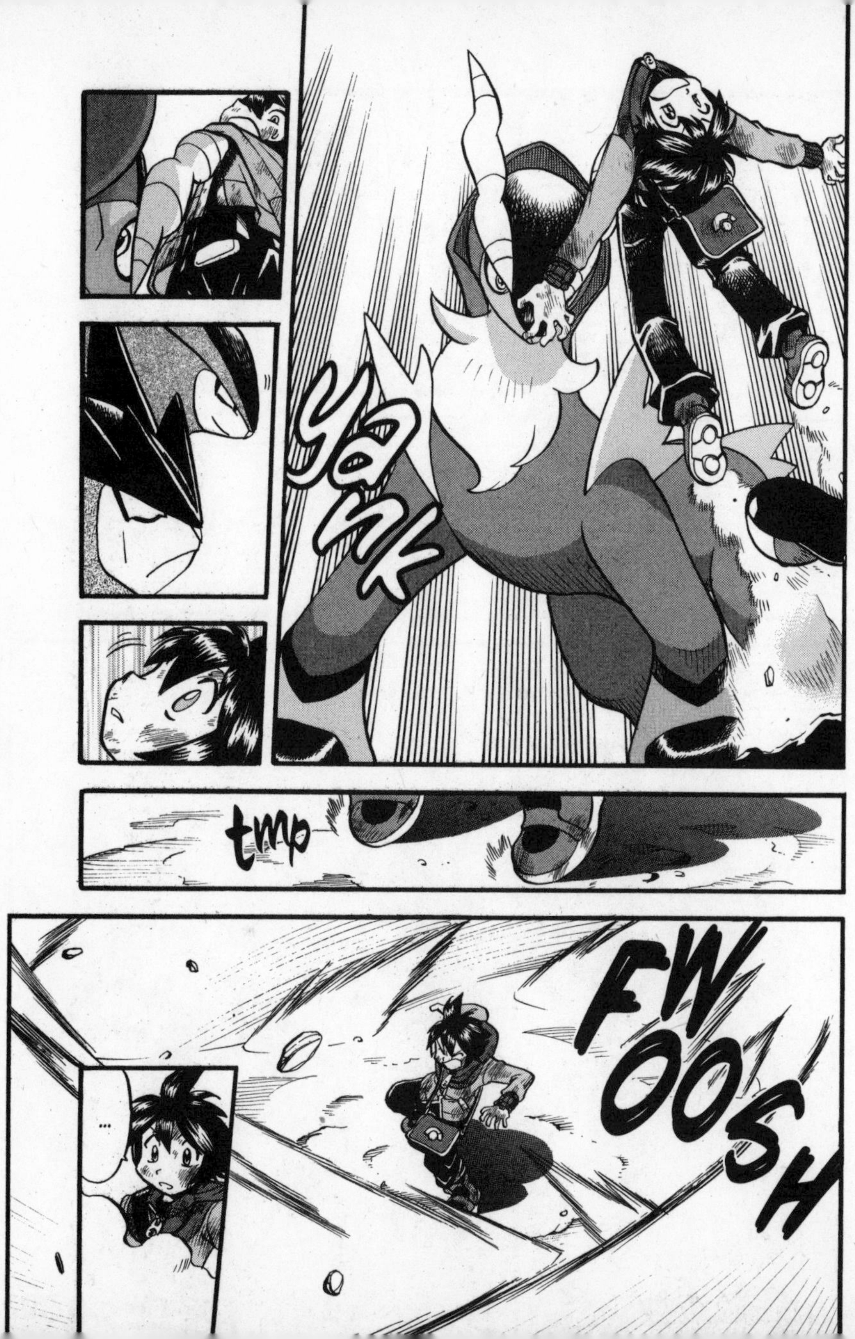
YANK
tmp
FWOOSH
...

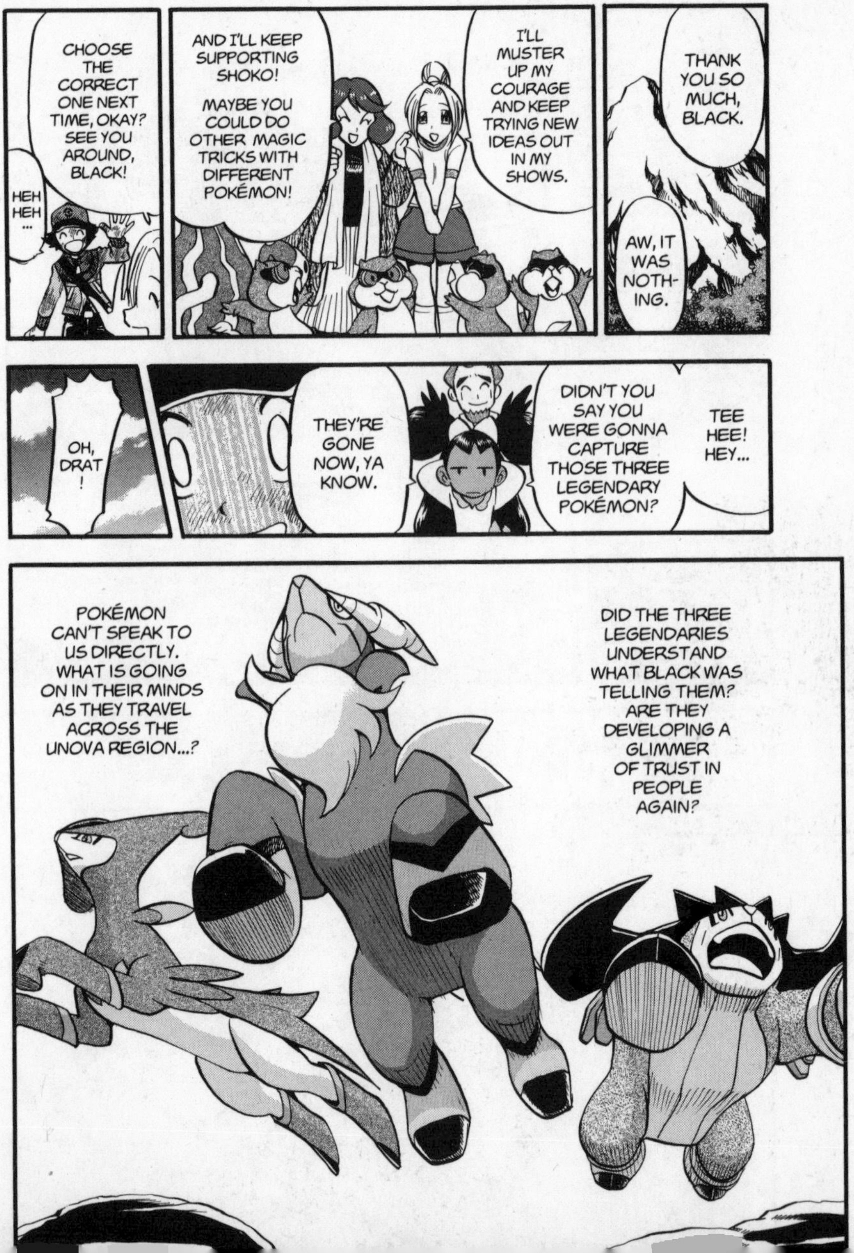
THANK YOU SO MUCH, BLACK.
AW, IT WAS NOTH-ING.
I'LL MUSTER UP MY COURAGE AND KEEP TRYING NEW IDEAS OUT IN MY SHOWS.
AND I'LL KEEP SUPPORTING SHOKO!
MAYBE YOU COULD DO OTHER MAGIC TRICKS WITH DIFFERENT POKÉMON!
CHOOSE THE CORRECT ONE NEXT TIME, OKAY? SEE YOU AROUND, BLACK!
HEH HEH ...
TEE HEE! HEY...
DIDN'T YOU SAY YOU WERE GONNA CAPTURE THOSE THREE LEGENDARY POKÉMON?
THEY'RE GONE NOW, YA KNOW.
OH, DRAT!
DID THE THREE LEGENDARIES UNDERSTAND WHAT BLACK WAS TELLING THEM? ARE THEY DEVELOPING A GLIMMER OF TRUST IN PEOPLE AGAIN?
POKÉMON CAN'T SPEAK TO US DIRECTLY. WHAT IS GOING ON IN THEIR MINDS AS THEY TRAVEL ACROSS THE UNOVA REGION...?

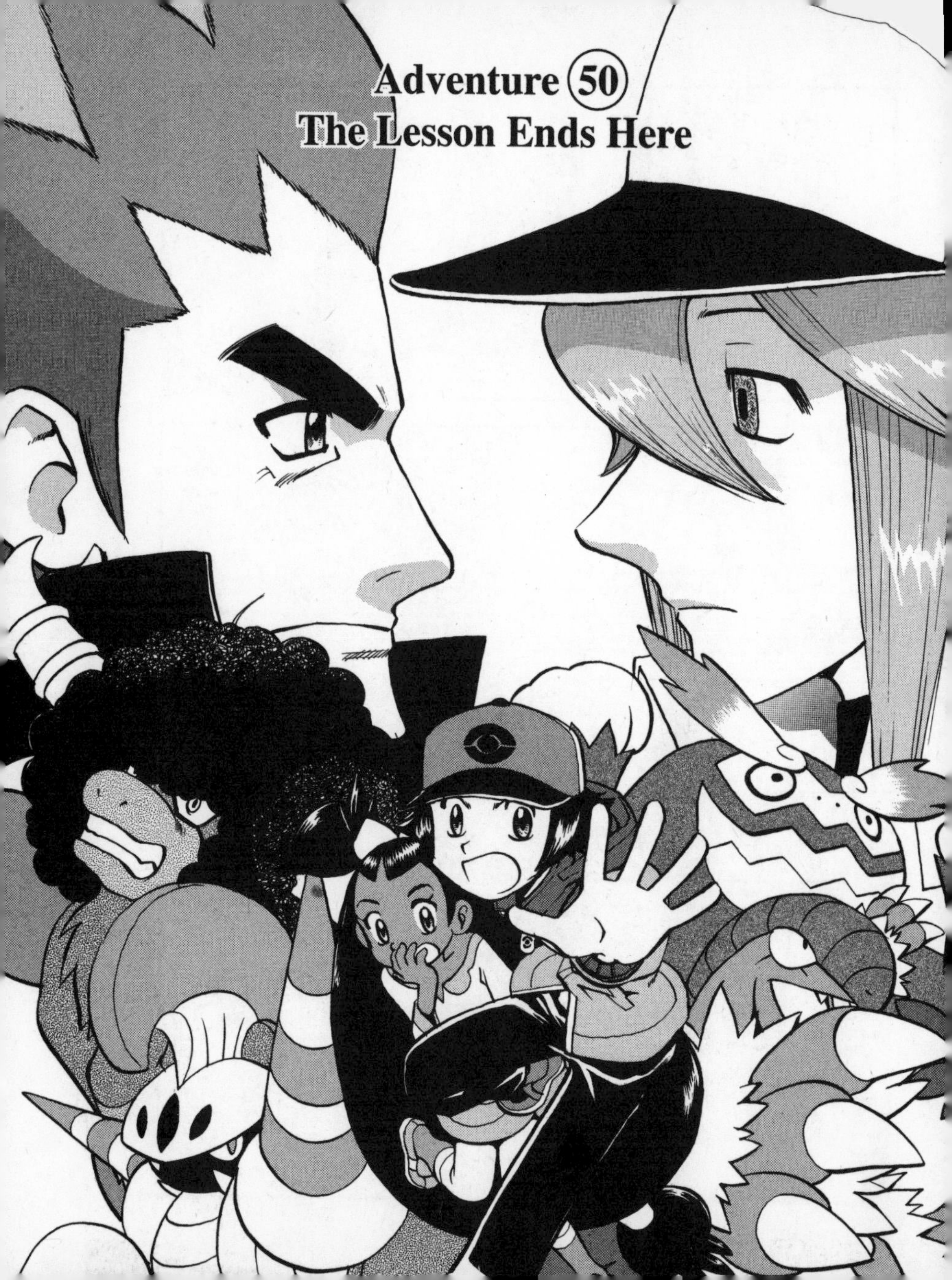
Adventure 50
The Lesson Ends Here

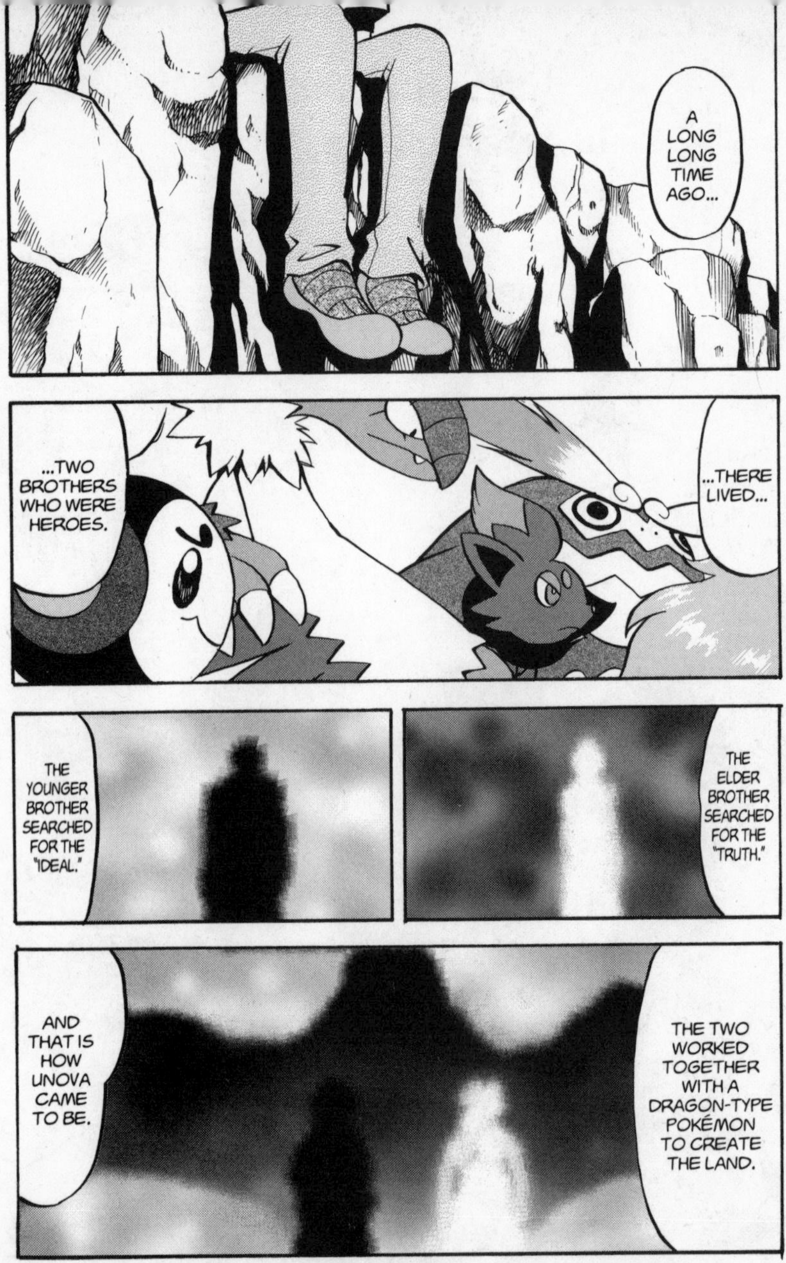
A LONG LONG TIME AGO...
...THERE LIVED...
...TWO BROTHERS WHO WERE HEROES.
THE ELDER BROTHER SEARCHED FOR THE "TRUTH."
THE YOUNGER BROTHER SEARCHED FOR THE "IDEAL."
THE TWO WORKED TOGETHER WITH A DRAGON-TYPE POKÉMON TO CREATE THE LAND.
AND THAT IS HOW UNOVA CAME TO BE.

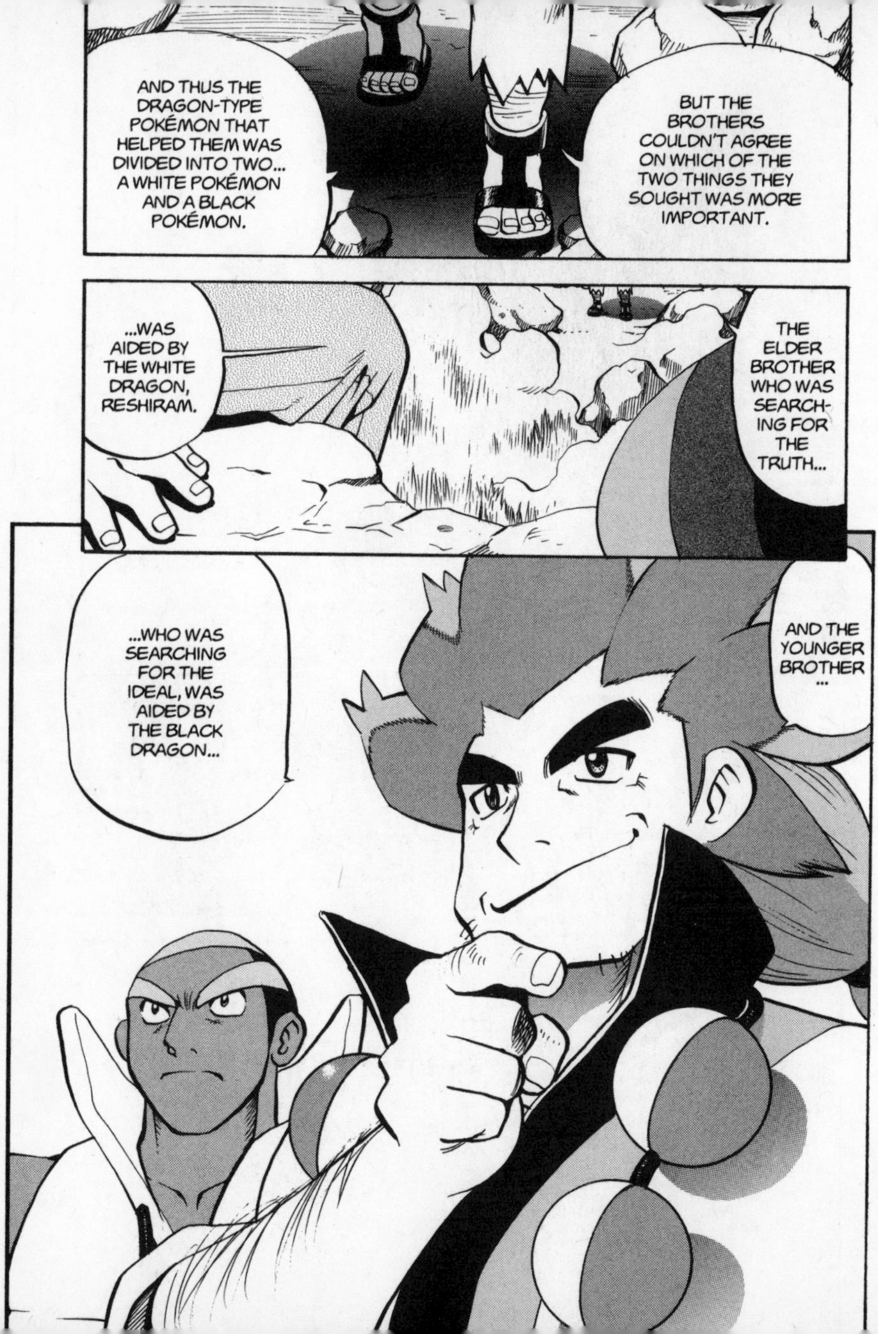
AND THUS THE DRAGON-TYPE POKÉMON THAT HELPED THEM WAS DIVIDED INTO TWO... A WHITE POKÉMON AND A BLACK POKÉMON.
BUT THE BROTHERS COULDN'T AGREE ON WHICH OF THE TWO THINGS THEY SOUGHT WAS MORE IMPORTANT.
THE ELDER BROTHER WHO WAS SEARCHING FOR THE TRUTH...
...WAS AIDED BY THE WHITE DRAGON, RESHIRAM.
AND THE YOUNGER BROTHER...
...WHO WAS SEARCHING FOR THE IDEAL, WAS AIDED BY THE BLACK DRAGON...

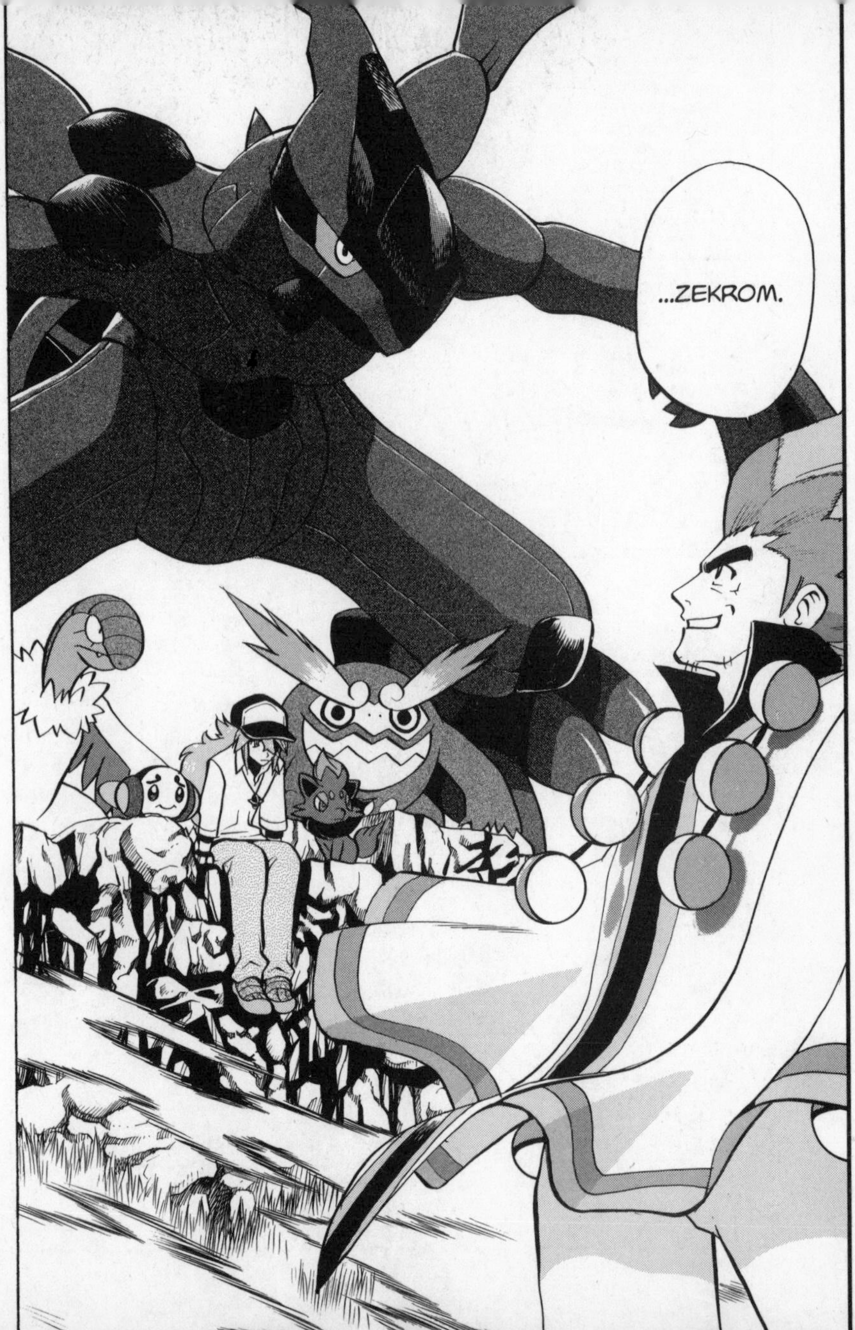
...ZEKROM.

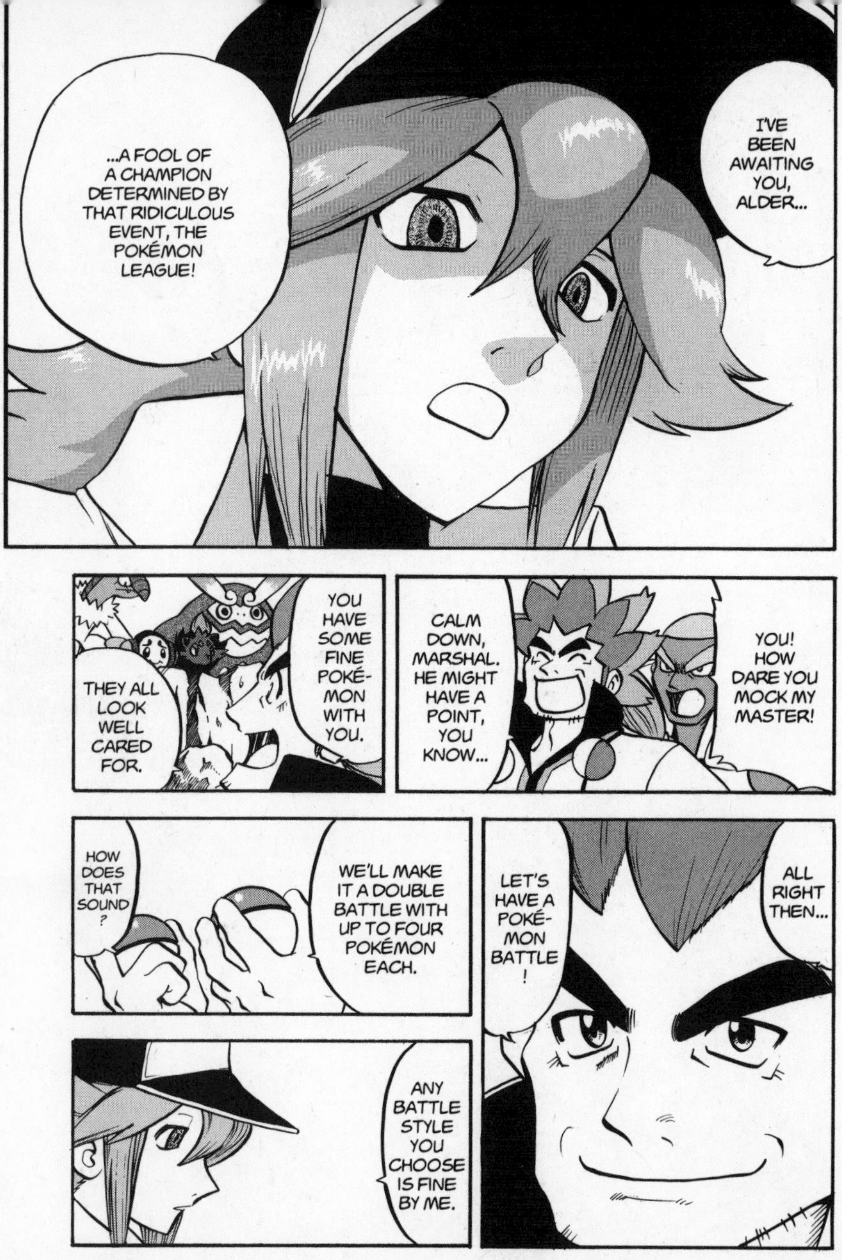
I'VE BEEN AWAITING YOU, ALDER...
...A FOOL OF A CHAMPION DETERMINED BY THAT RIDICULOUS EVENT, THE POKÉMON LEAGUE!
YOU! HOW DARE YOU MOCK MY MASTER!
CALM DOWN, MARSHAL. HE MIGHT HAVE A POINT, YOU KNOW...
YOU HAVE SOME FINE POKÉMON WITH YOU.
THEY ALL LOOK WELL CARED FOR.
ALL RIGHT THEN...
LET'S HAVE A POKÉMON BATTLE!
WE'LL MAKE IT A DOUBLE BATTLE WITH UP TO FOUR POKÉMON EACH.
HOW DOES THAT SOUND?
ANY BATTLE STYLE YOU CHOOSE IS FINE BY ME.

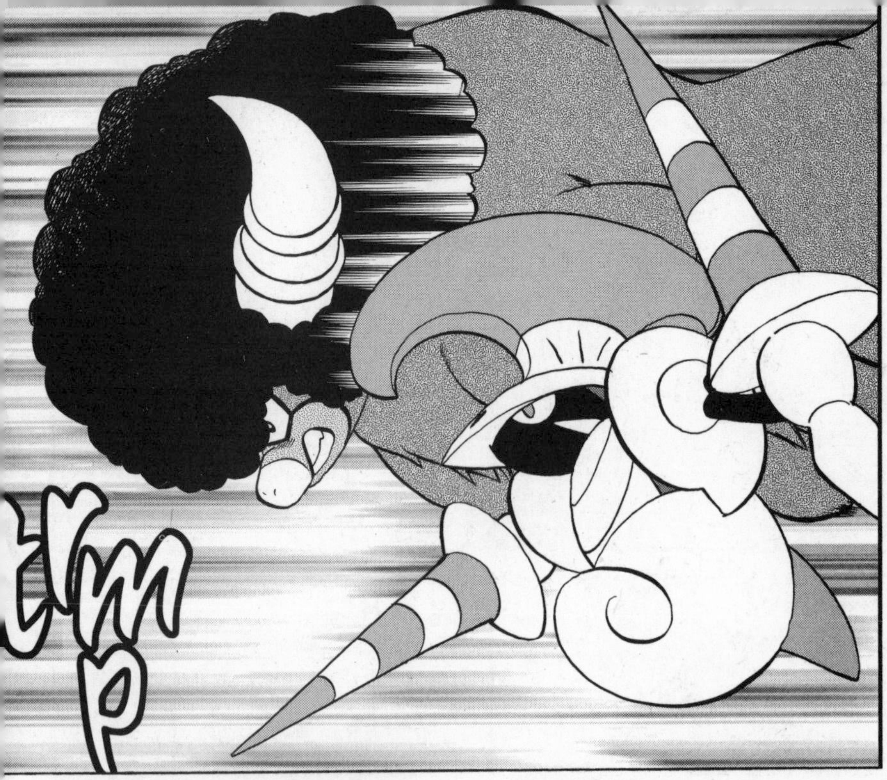

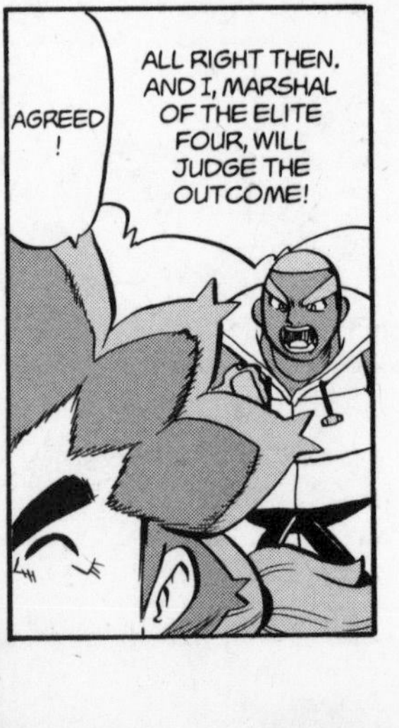
ALL RIGHT THEN. AND I, MARSHAL OF THE ELITE FOUR, WILL JUDGE THE OUTCOME!
AGREED!

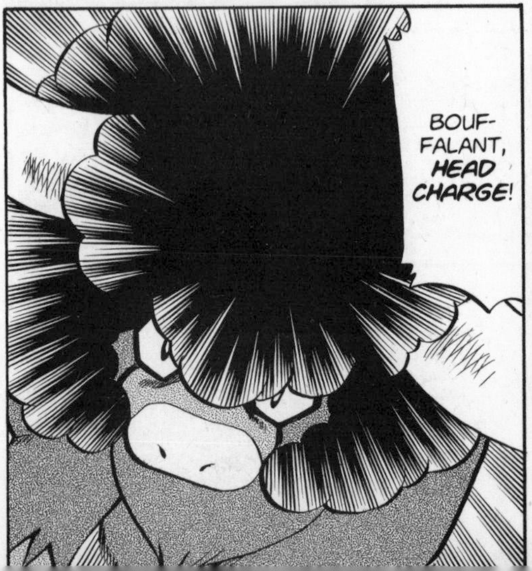
BOUF-FALANT, ***HEAD CHARGE***!

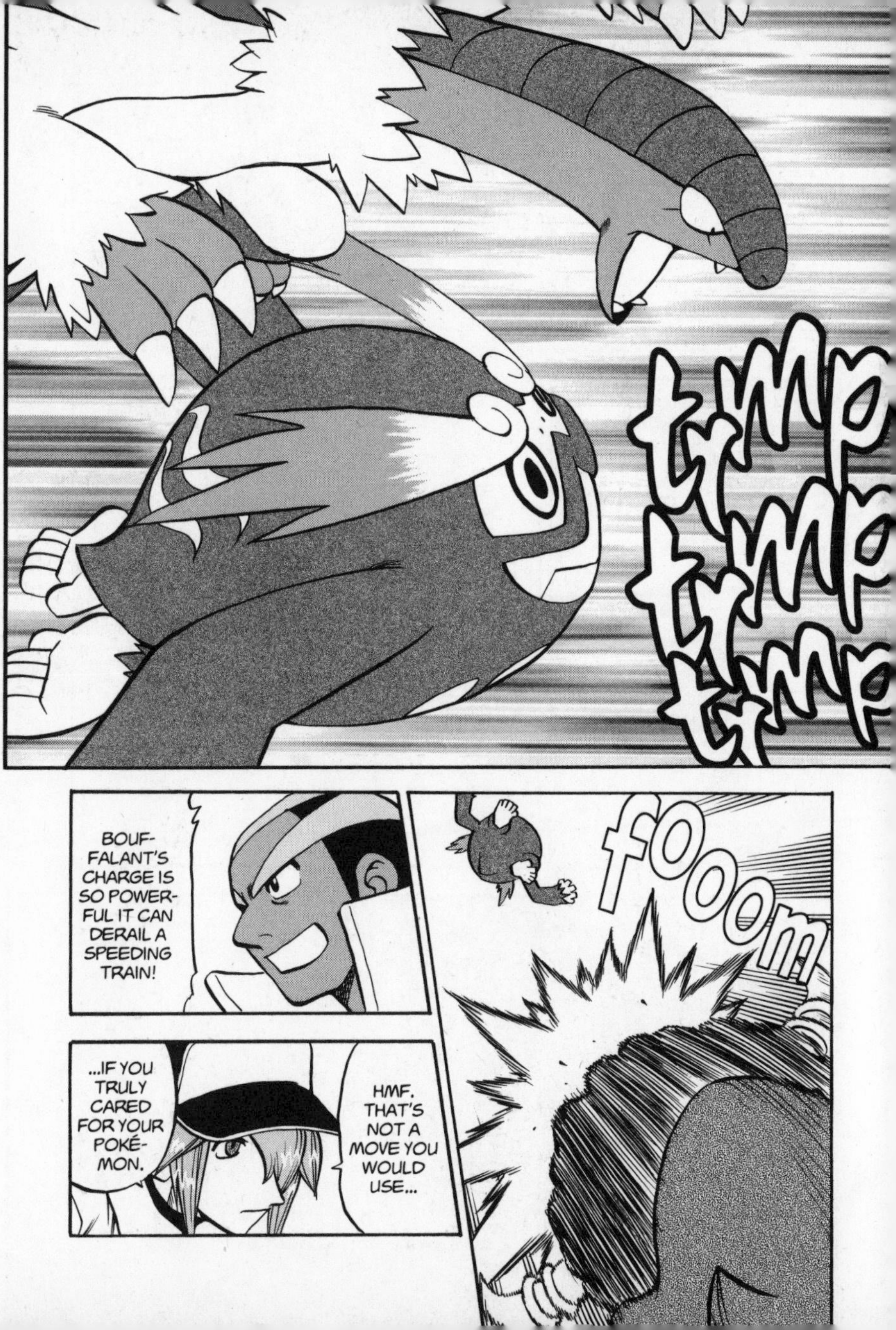
tmp
tmp
tmp
tmp
fooom
BOUF-FALANT'S CHARGE IS SO POWER-FUL IT CAN DERAIL A SPEEDING TRAIN!
HMF. THAT'S NOT A MOVE YOU WOULD USE...
...IF YOU TRULY CARED FOR YOUR POKÉ-MON.

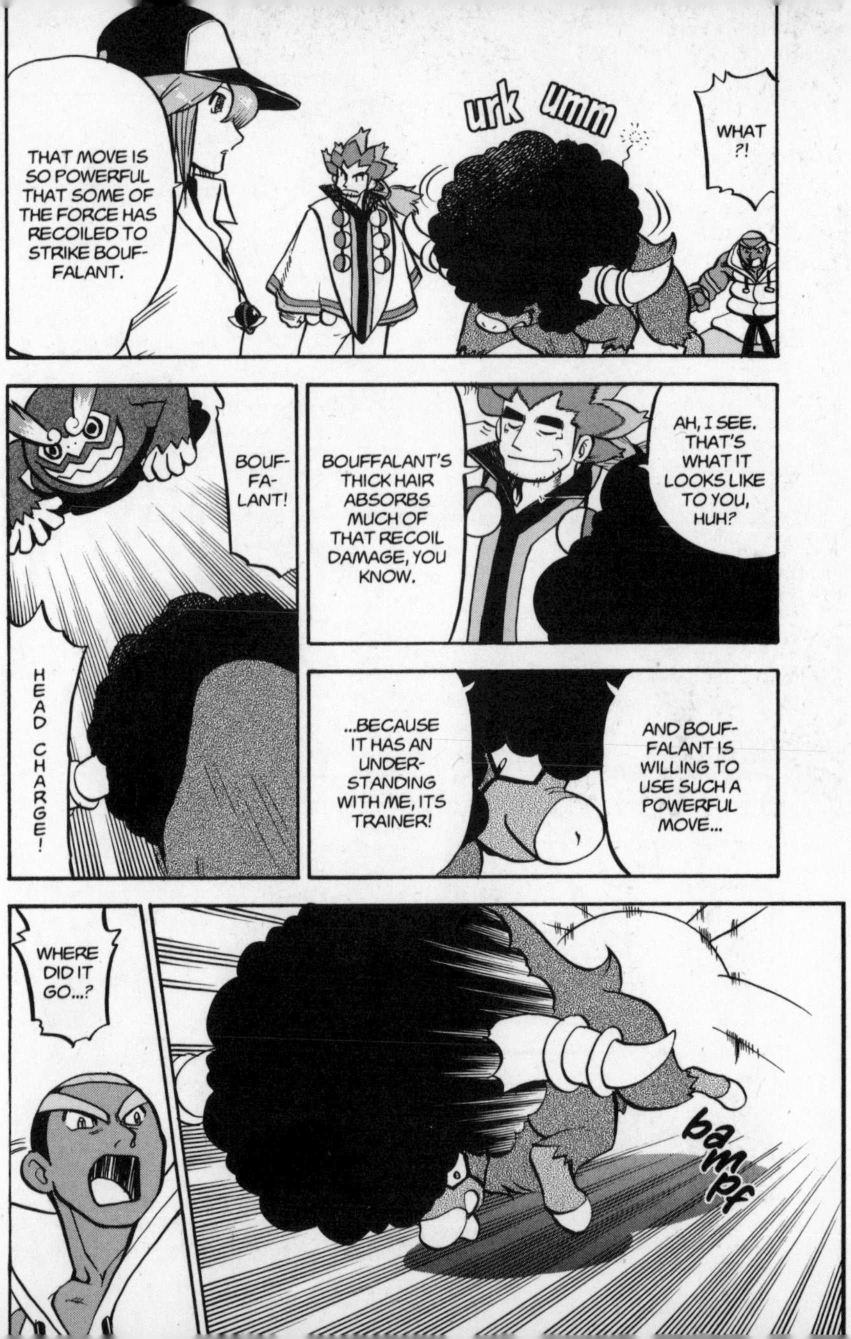
WHAT ?!
urk umm
THAT MOVE IS SO POWERFUL THAT SOME OF THE FORCE HAS RECOILED TO STRIKE BOUFFALANT.
AH, I SEE. THAT'S WHAT IT LOOKS LIKE TO YOU, HUH?
BOUFFALANT'S THICK HAIR ABSORBS MUCH OF THAT RECOIL DAMAGE, YOU KNOW.
AND BOUFFALANT IS WILLING TO USE SUCH A POWERFUL MOVE...
...BECAUSE IT HAS AN UNDERSTANDING WITH ME, ITS TRAINER!
BOUFFALANT!
HEAD CHARGE!
WHERE DID IT GO...?
bampf

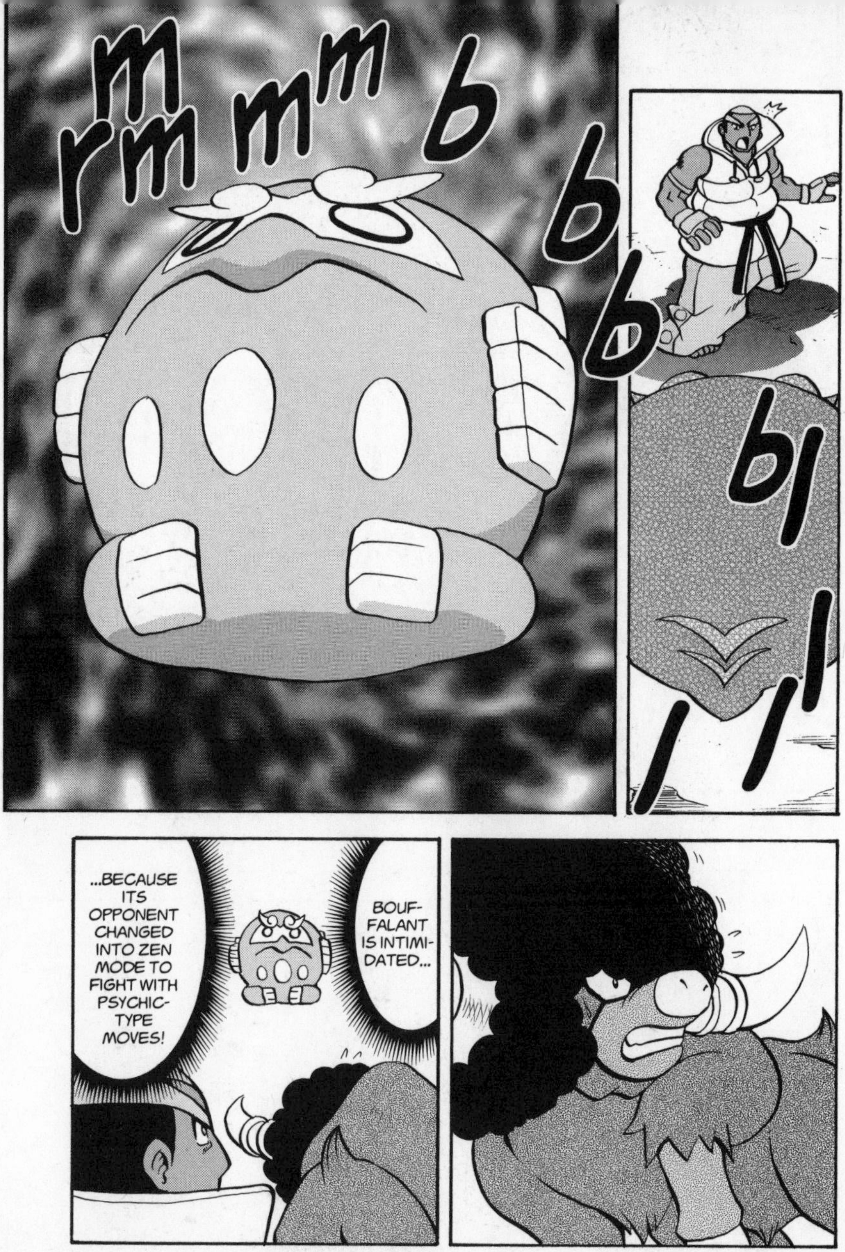
rmmmmmbbbbl
BOUFFALANT IS INTIMIDATED...
...BECAUSE ITS OPPONENT CHANGED INTO ZEN MODE TO FIGHT WITH PSYCHIC-TYPE MOVES!

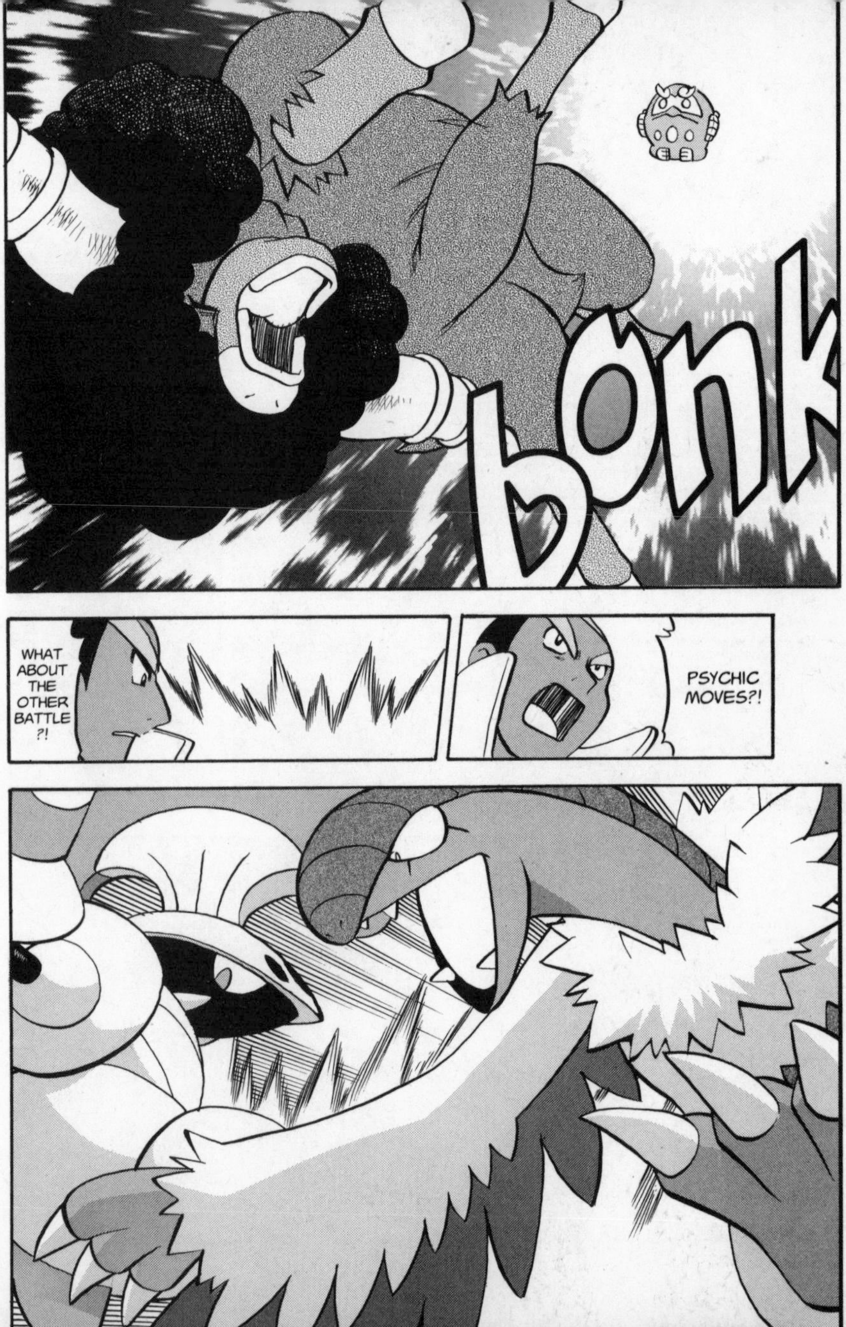
bonk
PSYCHIC MOVES?!
WHAT ABOUT THE OTHER BATTLE?!

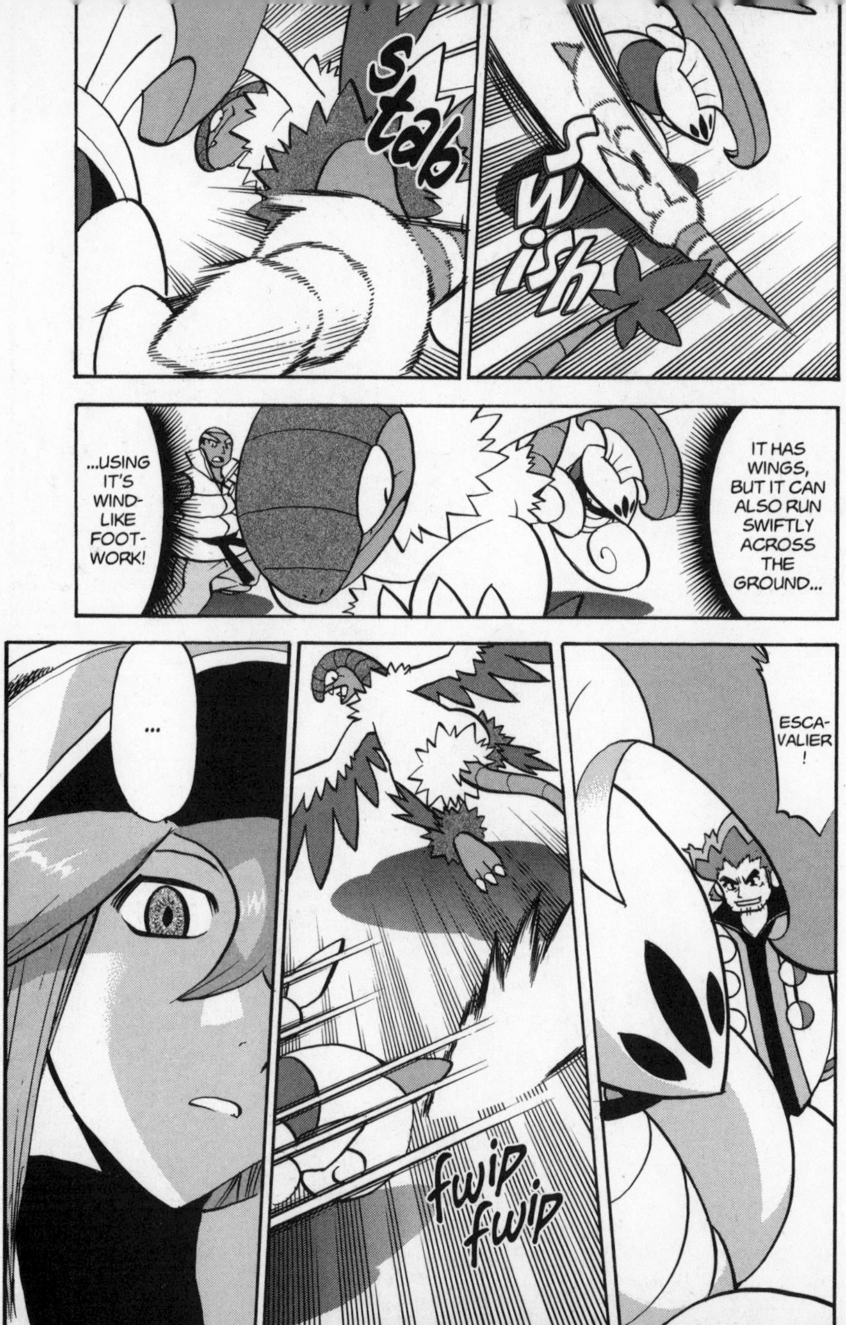
swish
stab
IT HAS WINGS, BUT IT CAN ALSO RUN SWIFTLY ACROSS THE GROUND...
...USING IT'S WIND-LIKE FOOTWORK!
ESCA-VALIER!
fwip fwip
...

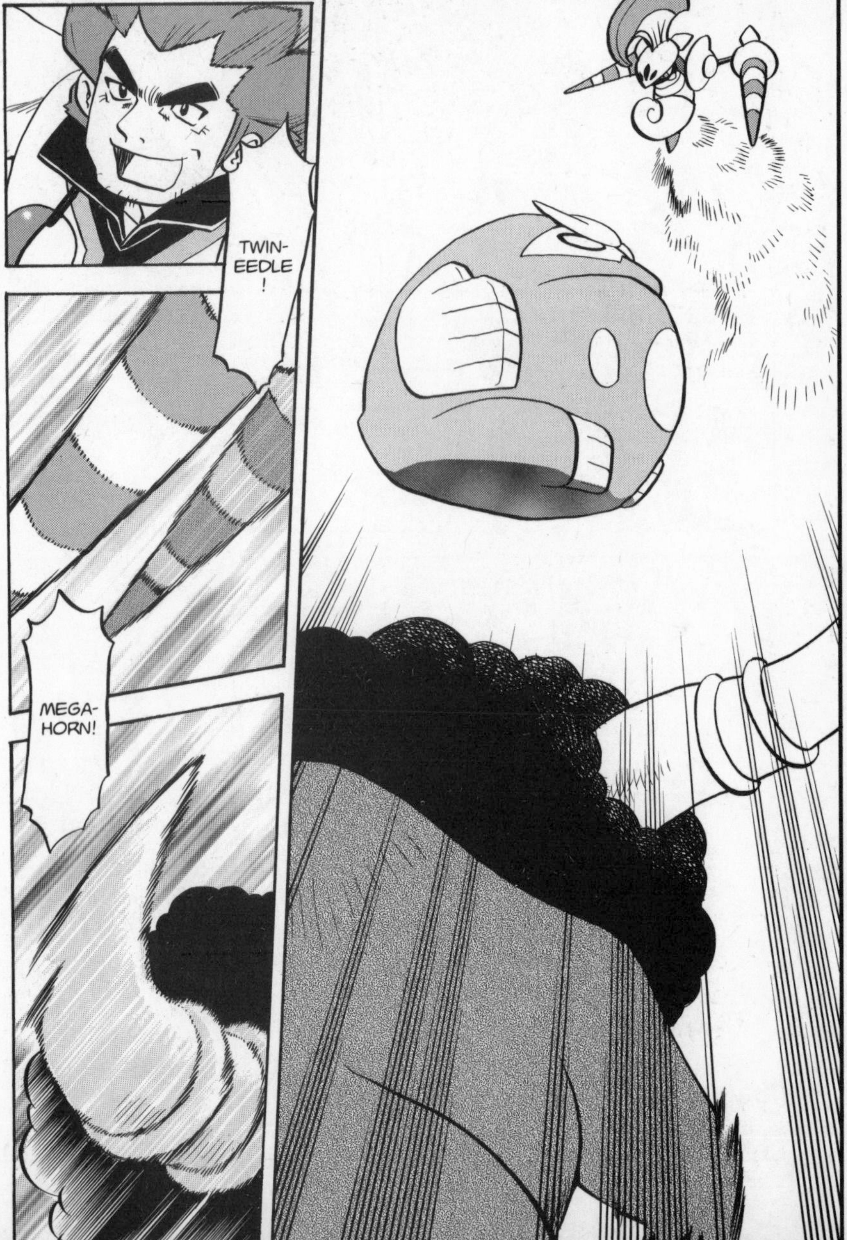
TWIN-EEDLE!
MEGA-HORN!

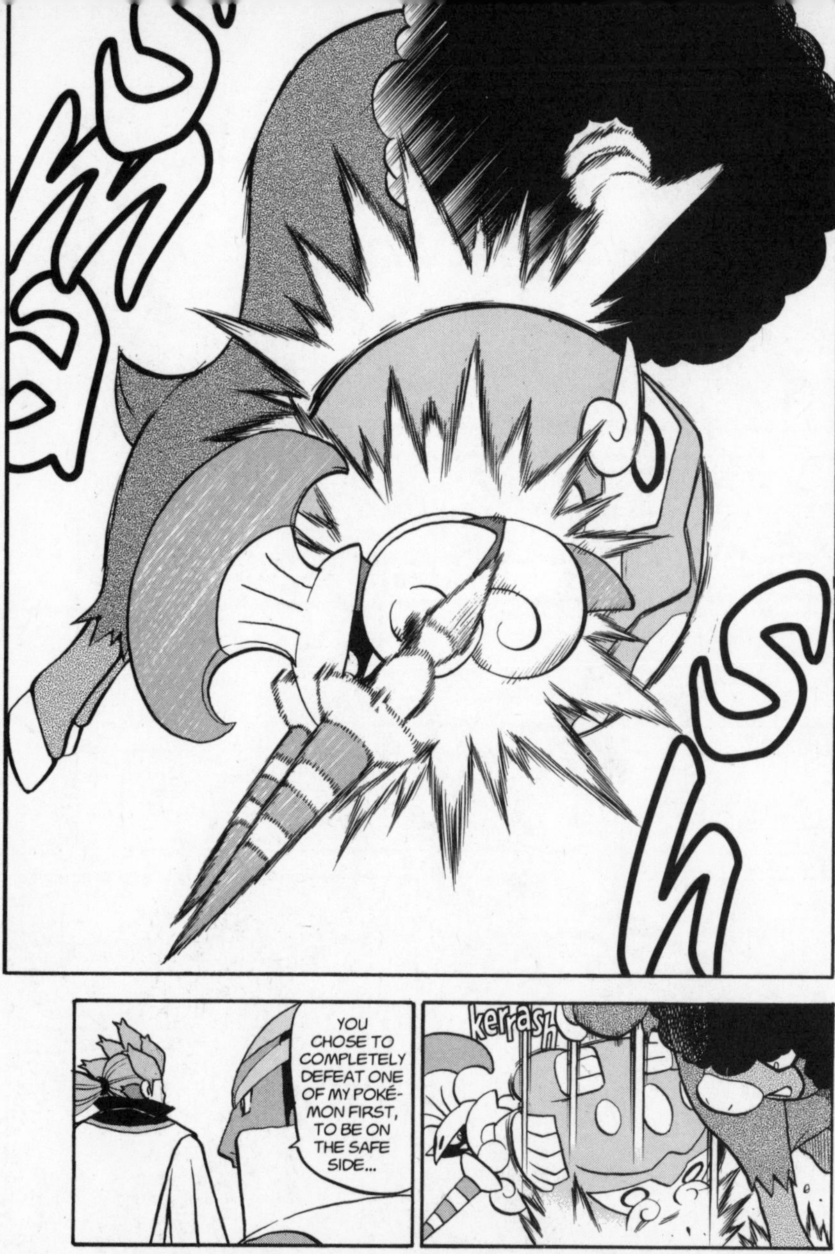
kerrash
YOU CHOSE TO COMPLETELY DEFEAT ONE OF MY POKÉ-MON FIRST, TO BE ON THE SAFE SIDE...

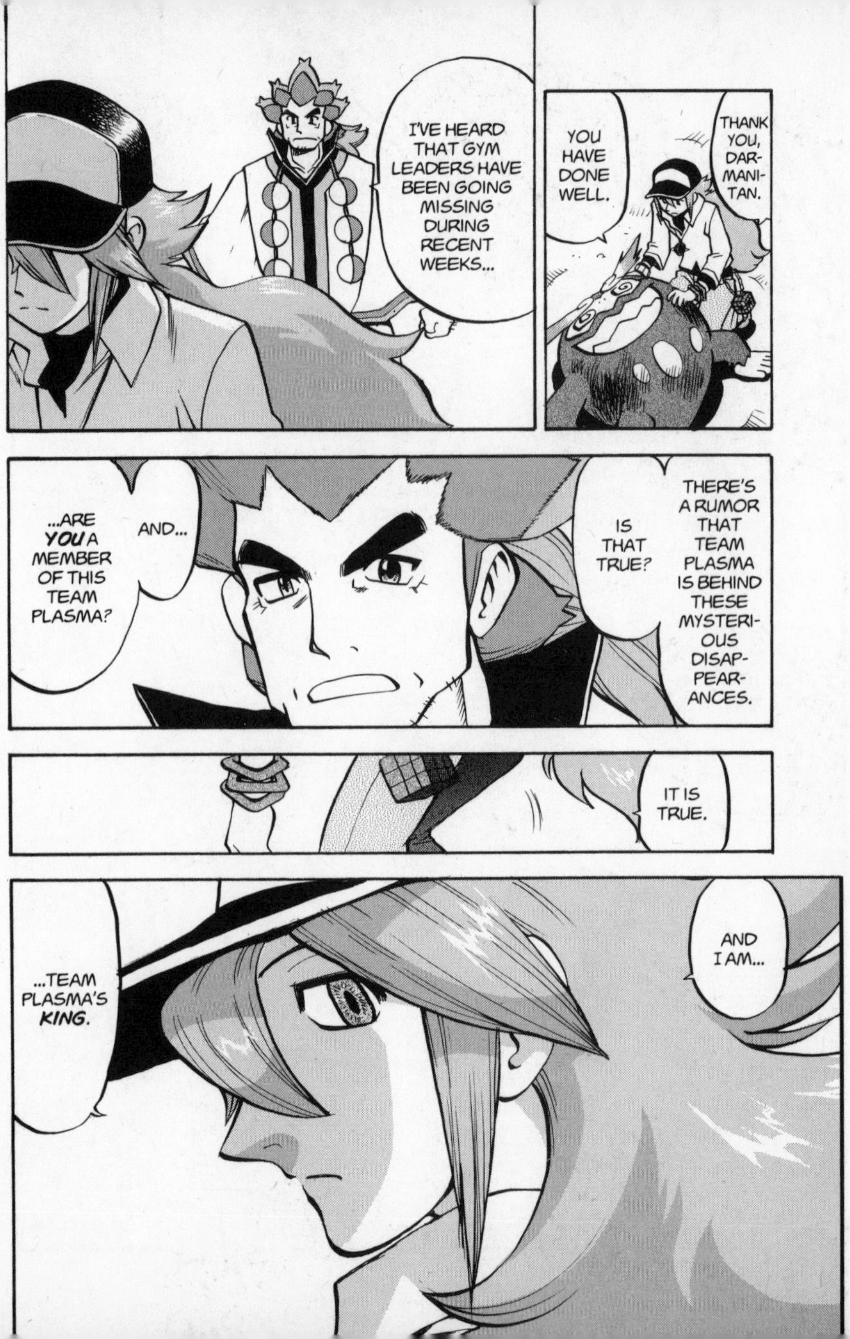
THANK YOU, DARMANITAN.
YOU HAVE DONE WELL.
I'VE HEARD THAT GYM LEADERS HAVE BEEN GOING MISSING DURING RECENT WEEKS...
THERE'S A RUMOR THAT TEAM PLASMA IS BEHIND THESE MYSTERIOUS DISAPPEARANCES.
IS THAT TRUE?
AND...
...ARE ***YOU*** A MEMBER OF THIS TEAM PLASMA?
IT IS TRUE.
AND I AM...
...TEAM PLASMA'S ***KING***.

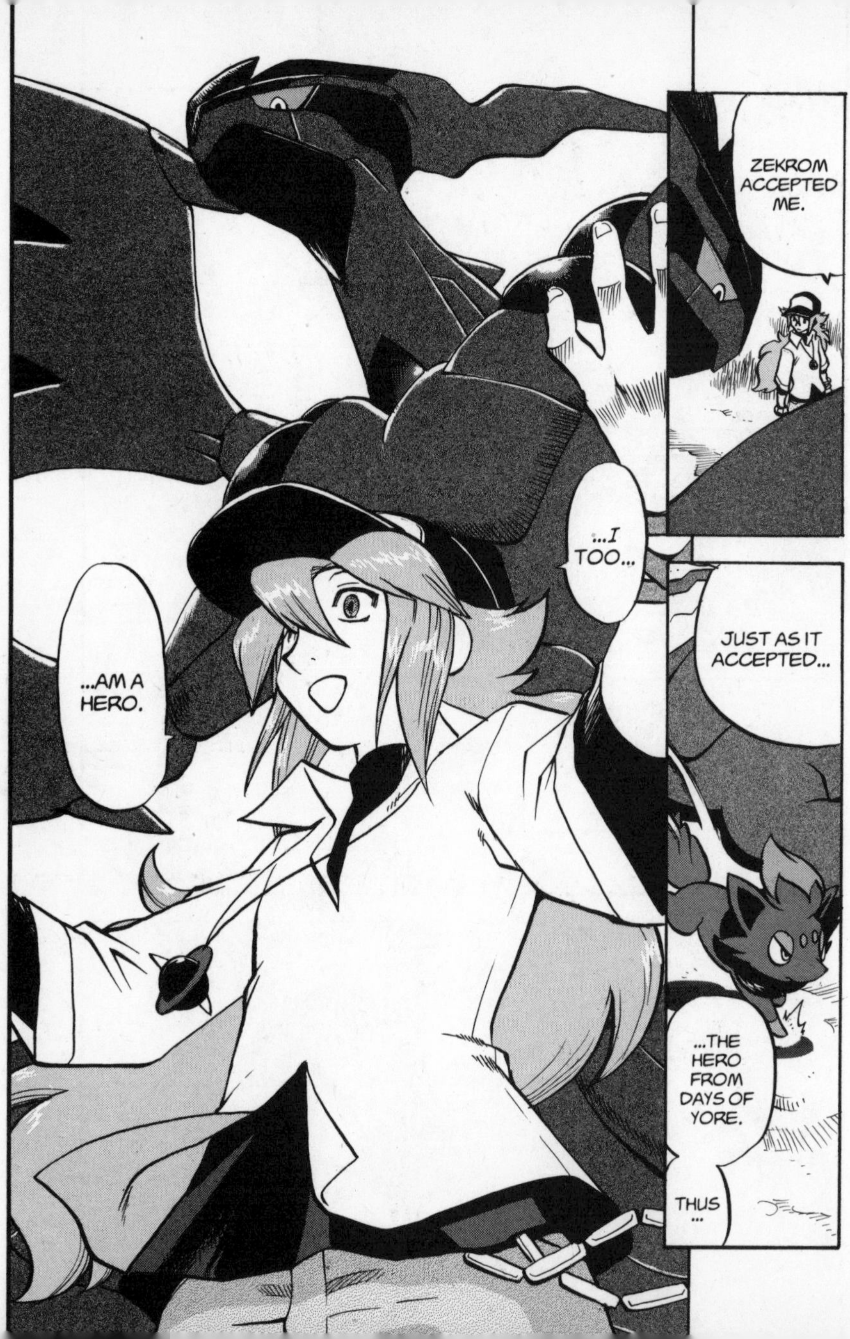
ZEKROM ACCEPTED ME.
JUST AS IT ACCEPTED...
...THE HERO FROM DAYS OF YORE.
THUS...
...I TOO...
...AM A HERO.

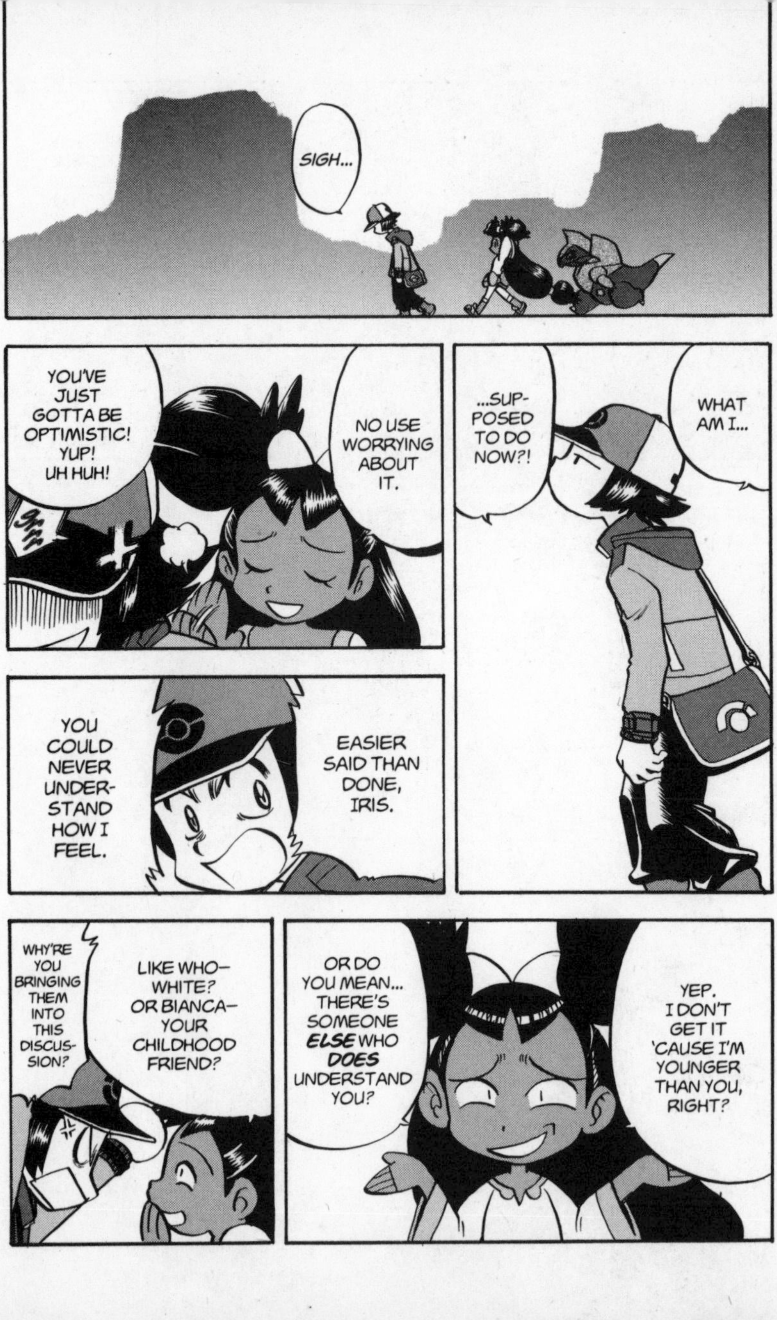
SIGH...
WHAT AM I...
...SUPPOSED TO DO NOW?!
NO USE WORRYING ABOUT IT.
YOU'VE JUST GOTTA BE OPTIMISTIC! YUP! UH HUH!
EASIER SAID THAN DONE, IRIS.
YOU COULD NEVER UNDERSTAND HOW I FEEL.
YEP. I DON'T GET IT 'CAUSE I'M YOUNGER THAN YOU, RIGHT?
OR DO YOU MEAN... THERE'S SOMEONE ELSE WHO DOES UNDERSTAND YOU?
LIKE WHO—WHITE? OR BIANCA—YOUR CHILDHOOD FRIEND?
WHY'RE YOU BRINGING THEM INTO THIS DISCUSSION?

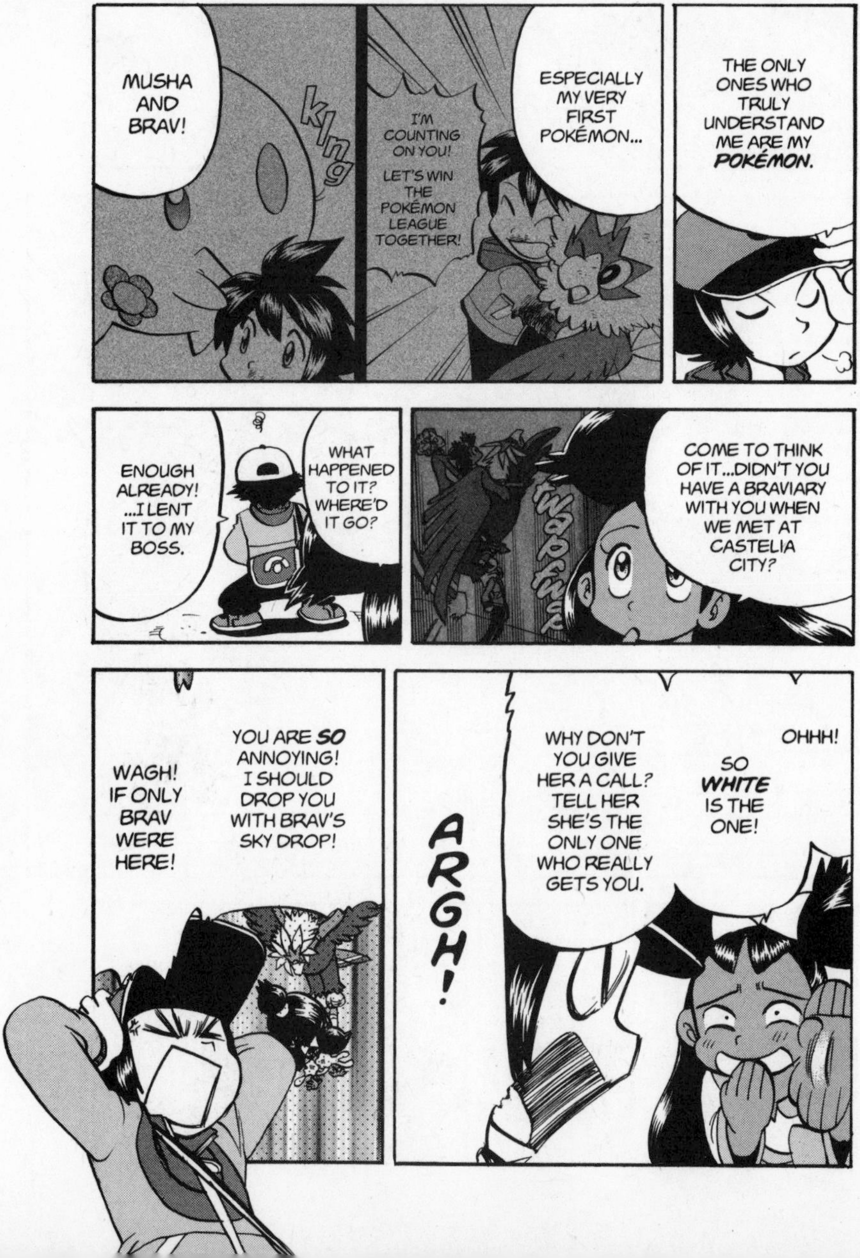
THE ONLY ONES WHO TRULY UNDERSTAND ME ARE MY ***POKÉMON.***
ESPECIALLY MY VERY FIRST POKÉMON...
I'M COUNTING ON YOU!
LET'S WIN THE POKÉMON LEAGUE TOGETHER!
kling
MUSHA AND BRAV!
COME TO THINK OF IT...DIDN'T YOU HAVE A BRAVIARY WITH YOU WHEN WE MET AT CASTELIA CITY?
WHAT HAPPENED TO IT? WHERE'D IT GO?
ENOUGH ALREADY! ...I LENT IT TO MY BOSS.
OHHH!
SO ***WHITE*** IS THE ONE!
WHY DON'T YOU GIVE HER A CALL? TELL HER SHE'S THE ONLY ONE WHO REALLY GETS YOU.
ARGH!
YOU ARE ***SO*** ANNOYING! I SHOULD DROP YOU WITH BRAV'S SKY DROP!
WAGH! IF ONLY BRAV WERE HERE!

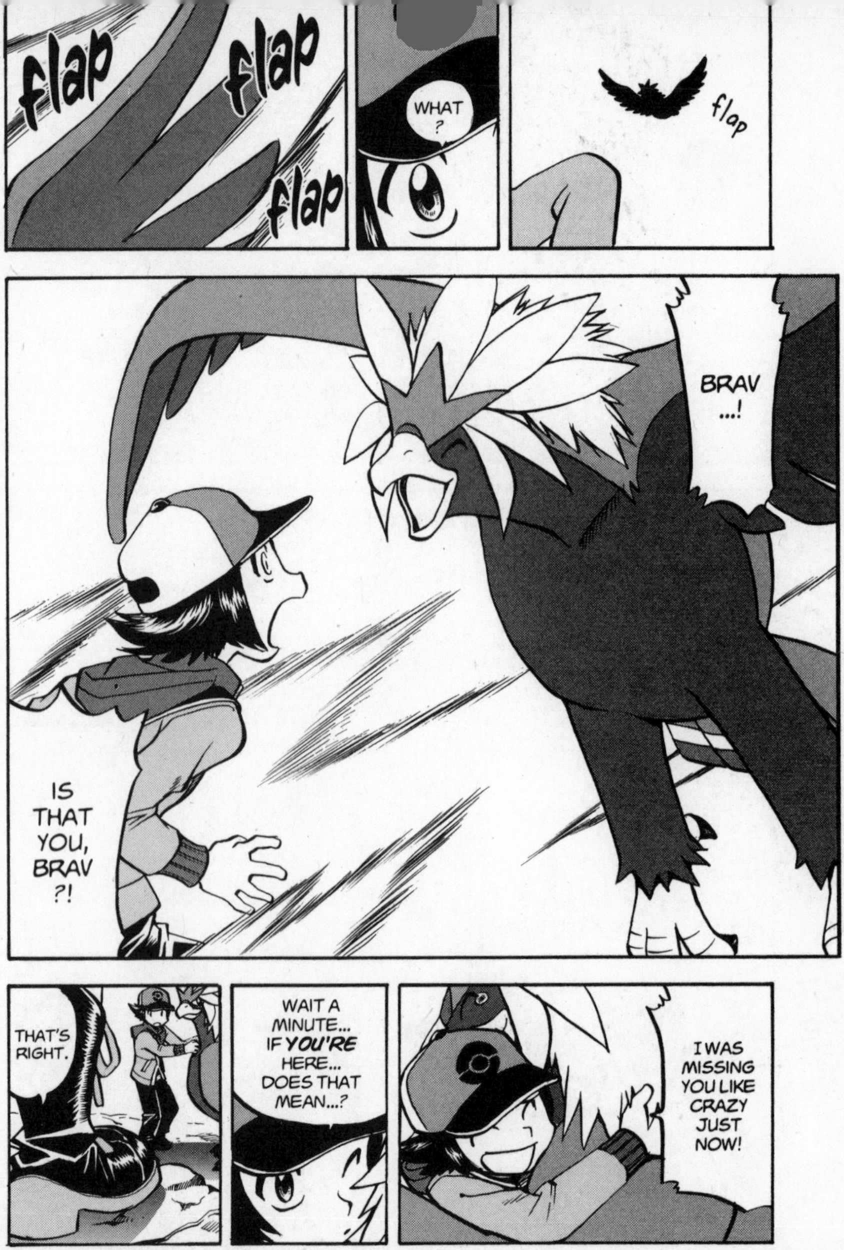
flap
WHAT ?
flap
flap
flap
BRAV ...!
IS THAT YOU, BRAV ?!
I WAS MISSING YOU LIKE CRAZY JUST NOW!
WAIT A MINUTE... IF **YOU'RE** HERE... DOES THAT MEAN...?
THAT'S RIGHT.

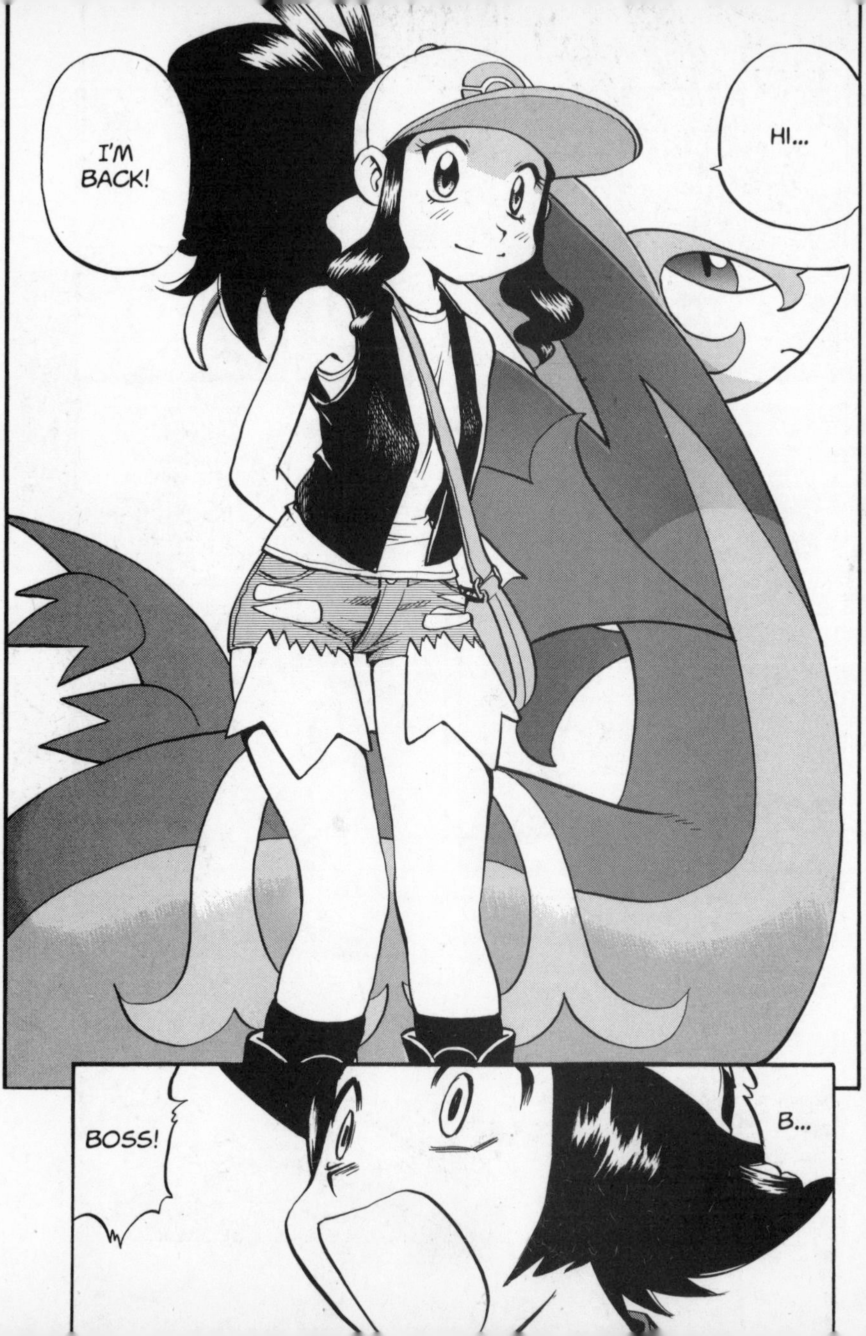
HI...
I'M BACK!
B...
BOSS!

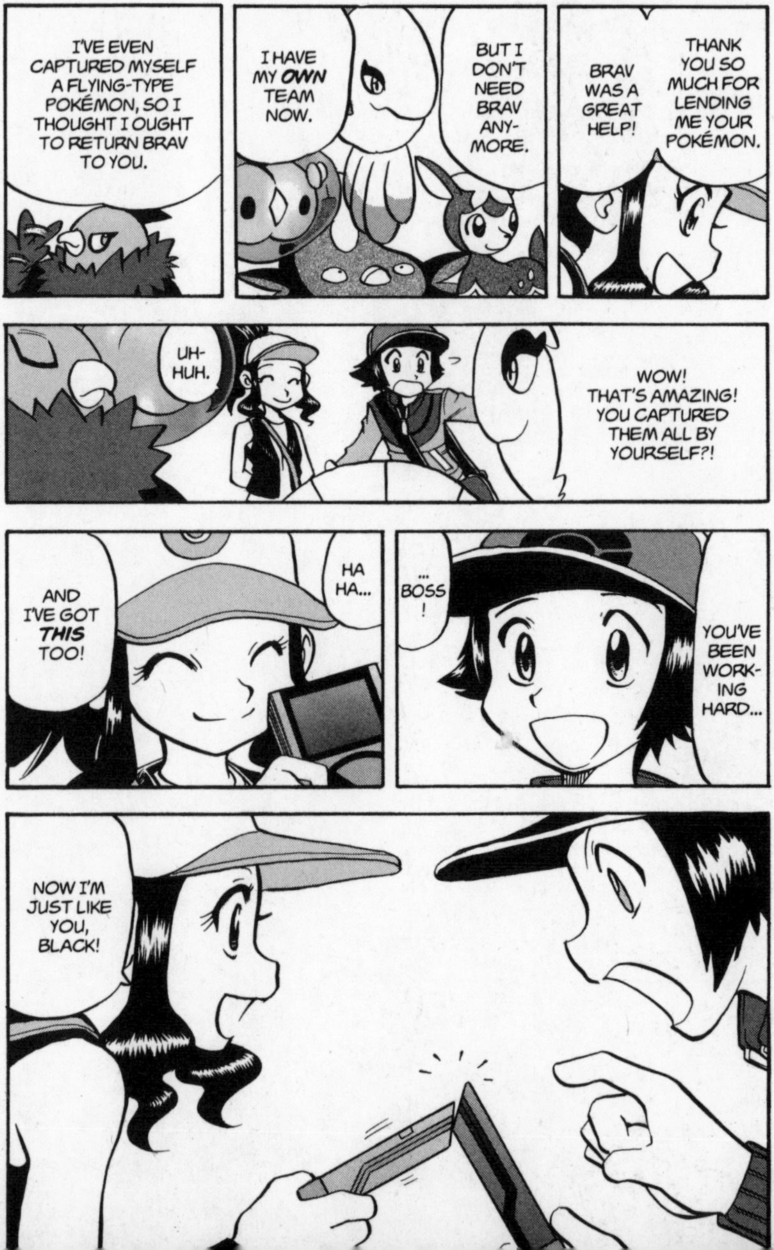
THANK YOU SO MUCH FOR LENDING ME YOUR POKÉMON.
BRAV WAS A GREAT HELP!
BUT I DON'T NEED BRAV ANYMORE.
I HAVE MY **OWN** TEAM NOW.
I'VE EVEN CAPTURED MYSELF A FLYING-TYPE POKÉMON, SO I THOUGHT I OUGHT TO RETURN BRAV TO YOU.
WOW! THAT'S AMAZING! YOU CAPTURED THEM ALL BY YOURSELF?!
UH-HUH.
YOU'VE BEEN WORKING HARD...
...BOSS!
HA HA...
AND I'VE GOT **THIS** TOO!
NOW I'M JUST LIKE YOU, BLACK!

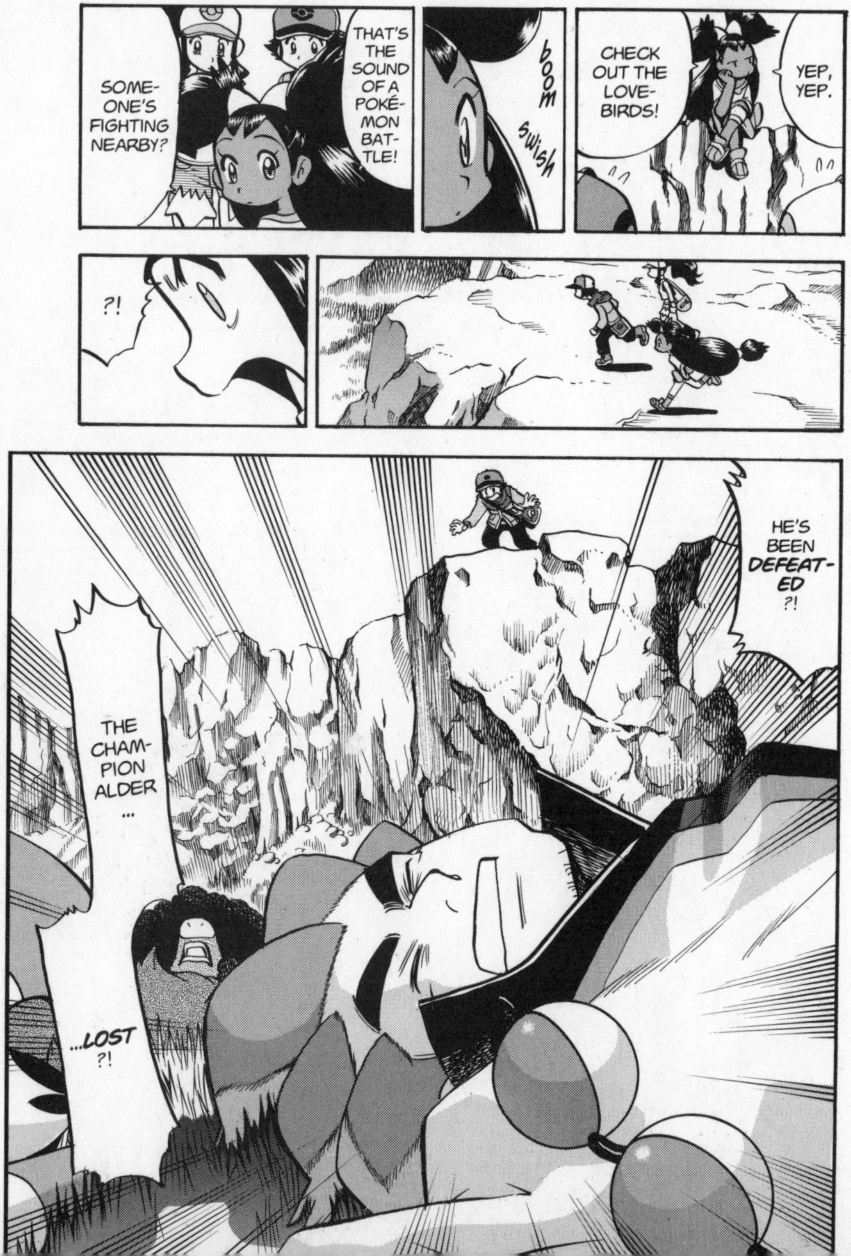
YEP, YEP.
CHECK OUT THE LOVE-BIRDS!
boom
swish
THAT'S THE SOUND OF A POKÉMON BATTLE!
SOME-ONE'S FIGHTING NEARBY?
?!
HE'S BEEN *DEFEATED*?!
THE CHAMPION ALDER...
...*LOST*?!

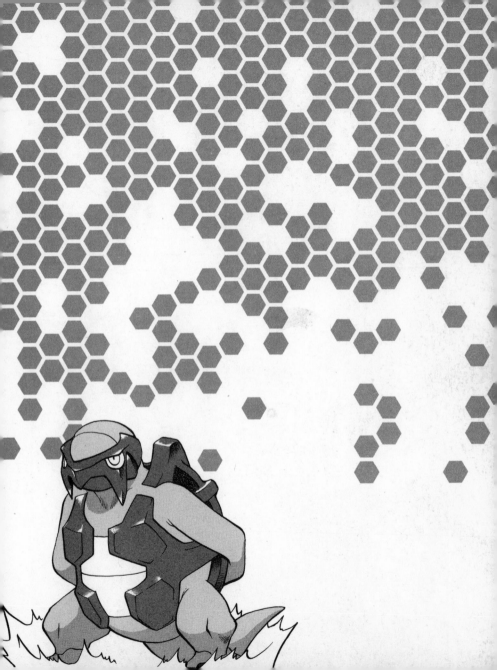

Adventure 51
Will the Truth Come Out?

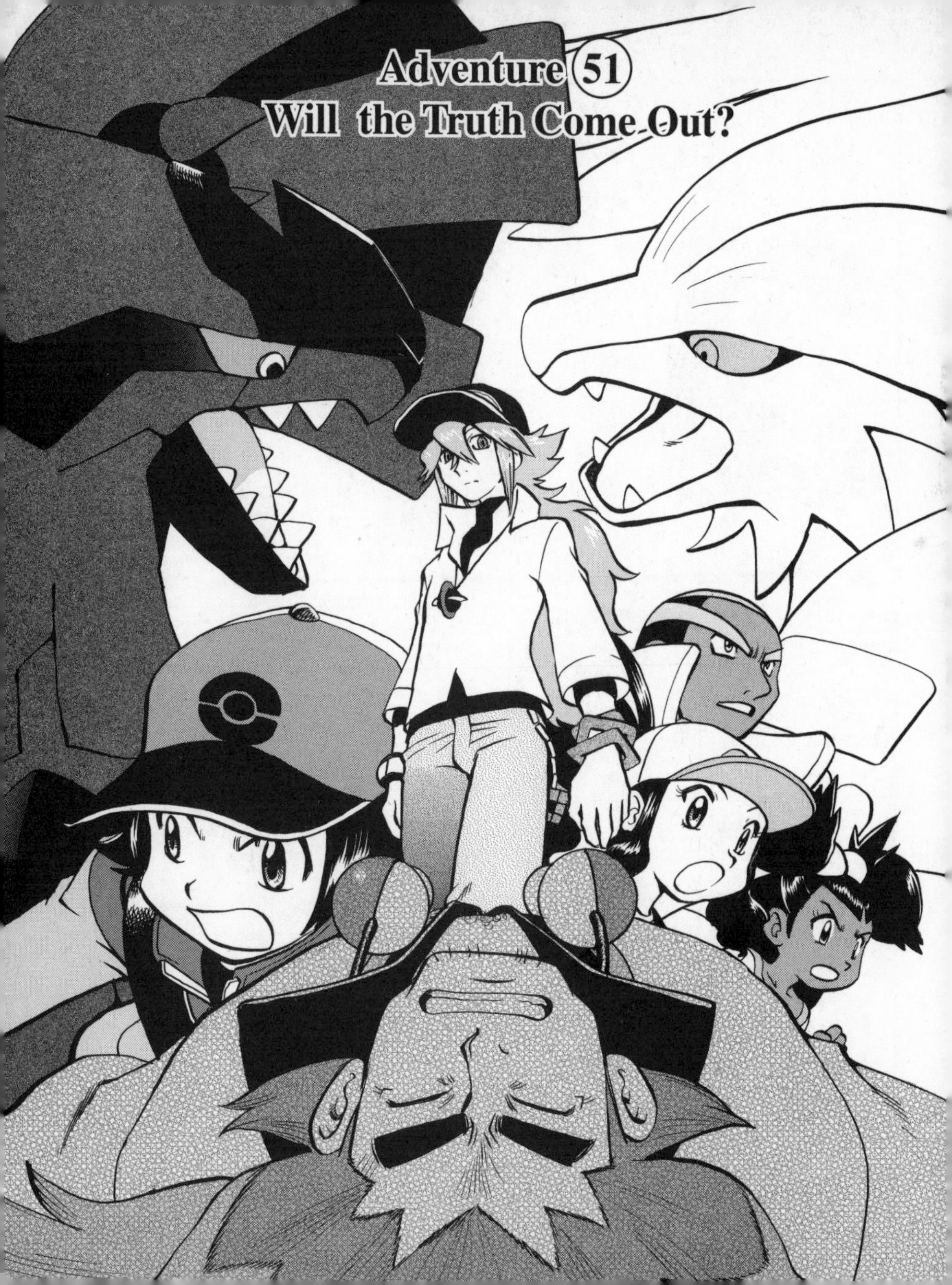

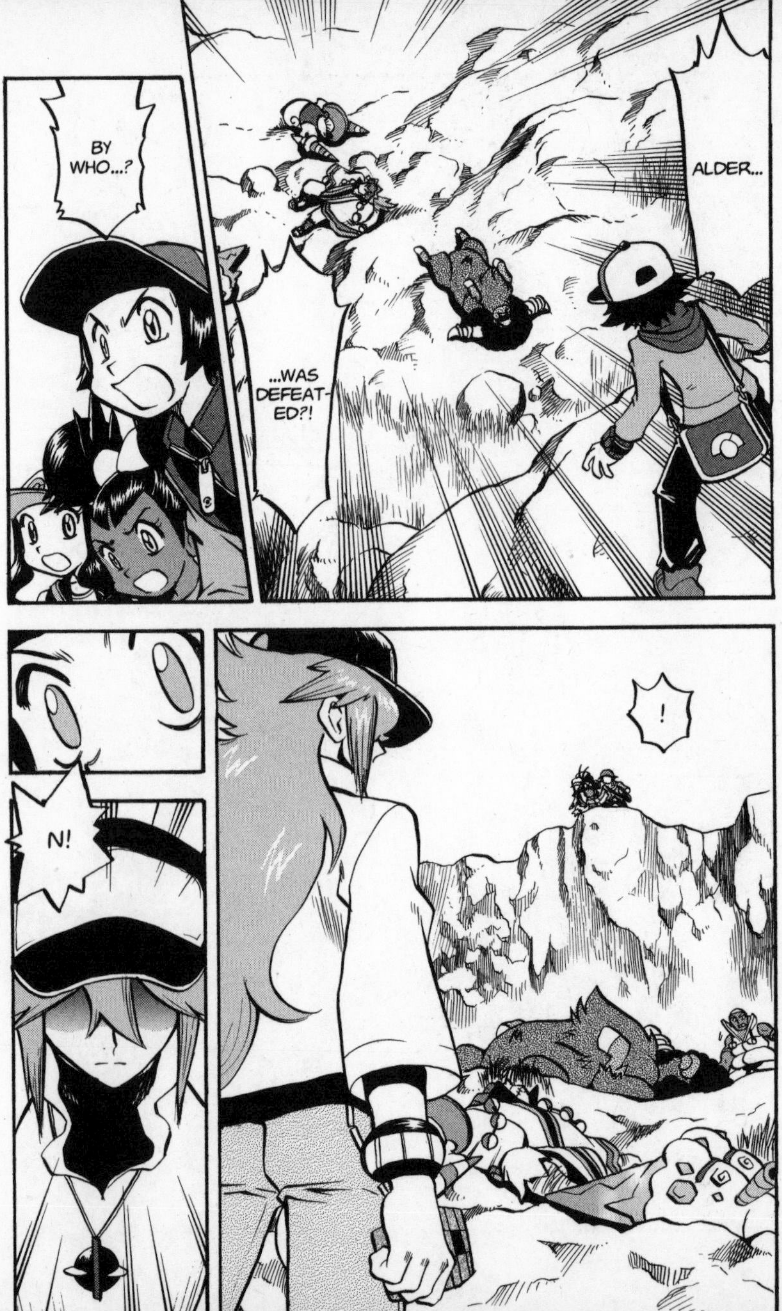
ALDER...
...WAS DEFEAT-ED?!
BY WHO...?
!
N!

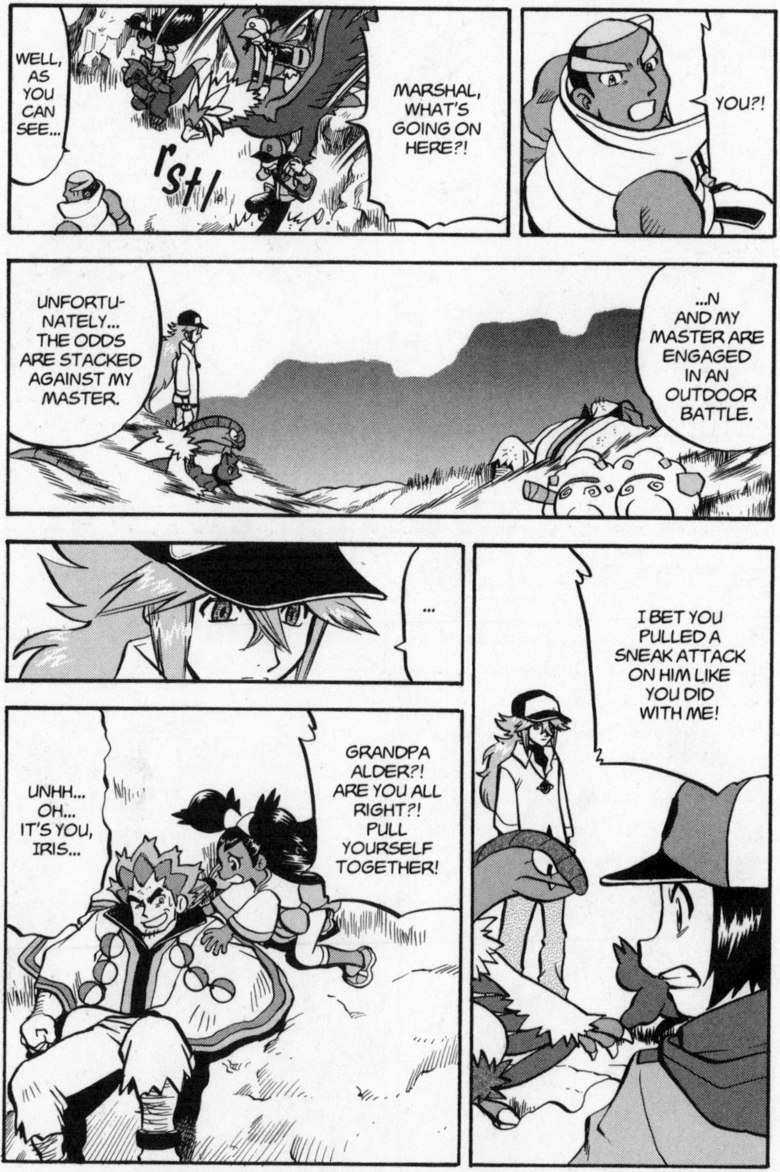
YOU?!
MARSHAL, WHAT'S GOING ON HERE?!
WELL, AS YOU CAN SEE...
rst/
...N AND MY MASTER ARE ENGAGED IN AN OUTDOOR BATTLE.
UNFORTU-NATELY... THE ODDS ARE STACKED AGAINST MY MASTER.
I BET YOU PULLED A SNEAK ATTACK ON HIM LIKE YOU DID WITH ME!
...
GRANDPA ALDER?! ARE YOU ALL RIGHT?! PULL YOURSELF TOGETHER!
UNHH... OH... IT'S YOU, IRIS...

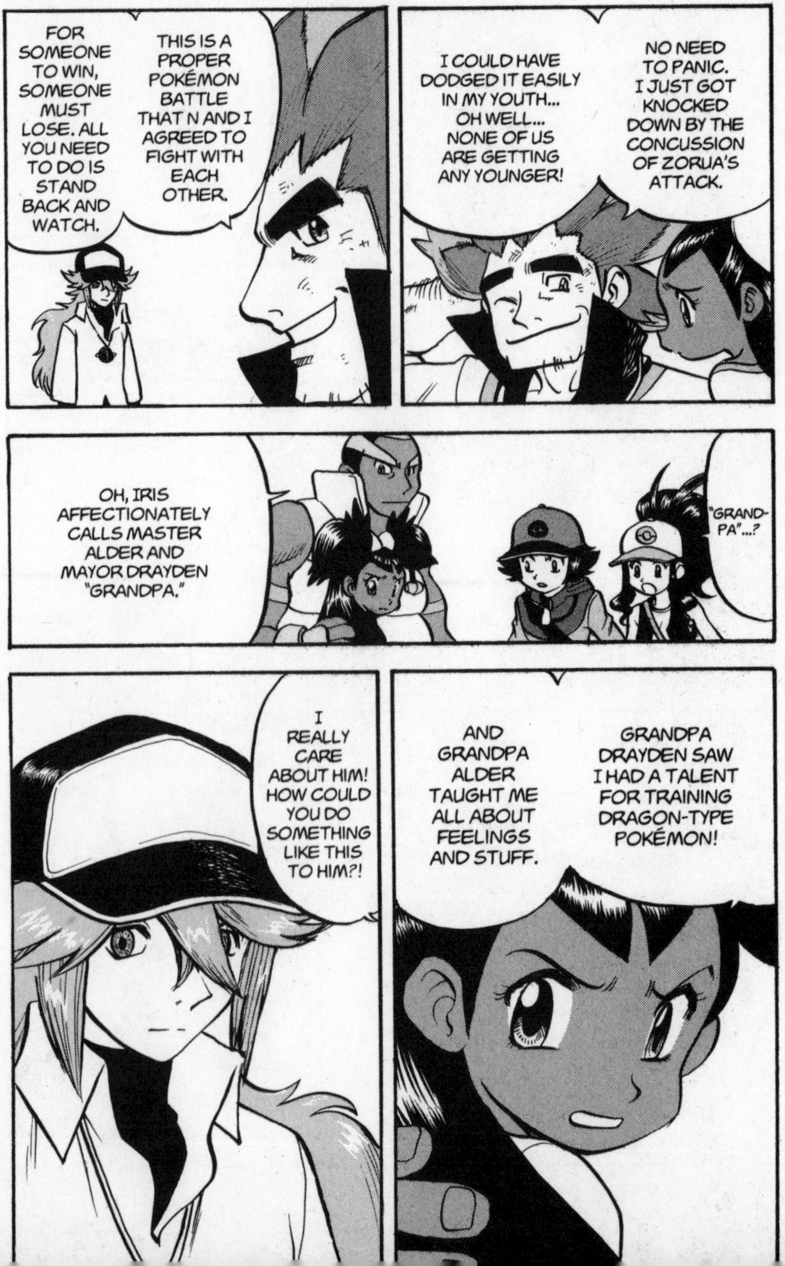
NO NEED TO PANIC. I JUST GOT KNOCKED DOWN BY THE CONCUSSION OF ZORUA'S ATTACK.
I COULD HAVE DODGED IT EASILY IN MY YOUTH... OH WELL... NONE OF US ARE GETTING ANY YOUNGER!
THIS IS A PROPER POKÉMON BATTLE THAT N AND I AGREED TO FIGHT WITH EACH OTHER.
FOR SOMEONE TO WIN, SOMEONE MUST LOSE. ALL YOU NEED TO DO IS STAND BACK AND WATCH.
"GRANDPA"...?
OH, IRIS AFFECTIONATELY CALLS MASTER ALDER AND MAYOR DRAYDEN "GRANDPA."
GRANDPA DRAYDEN SAW I HAD A TALENT FOR TRAINING DRAGON-TYPE POKÉMON!
AND GRANDPA ALDER TAUGHT ME ALL ABOUT FEELINGS AND STUFF.
I REALLY CARE ABOUT HIM! HOW COULD YOU DO SOMETHING LIKE THIS TO HIM?!

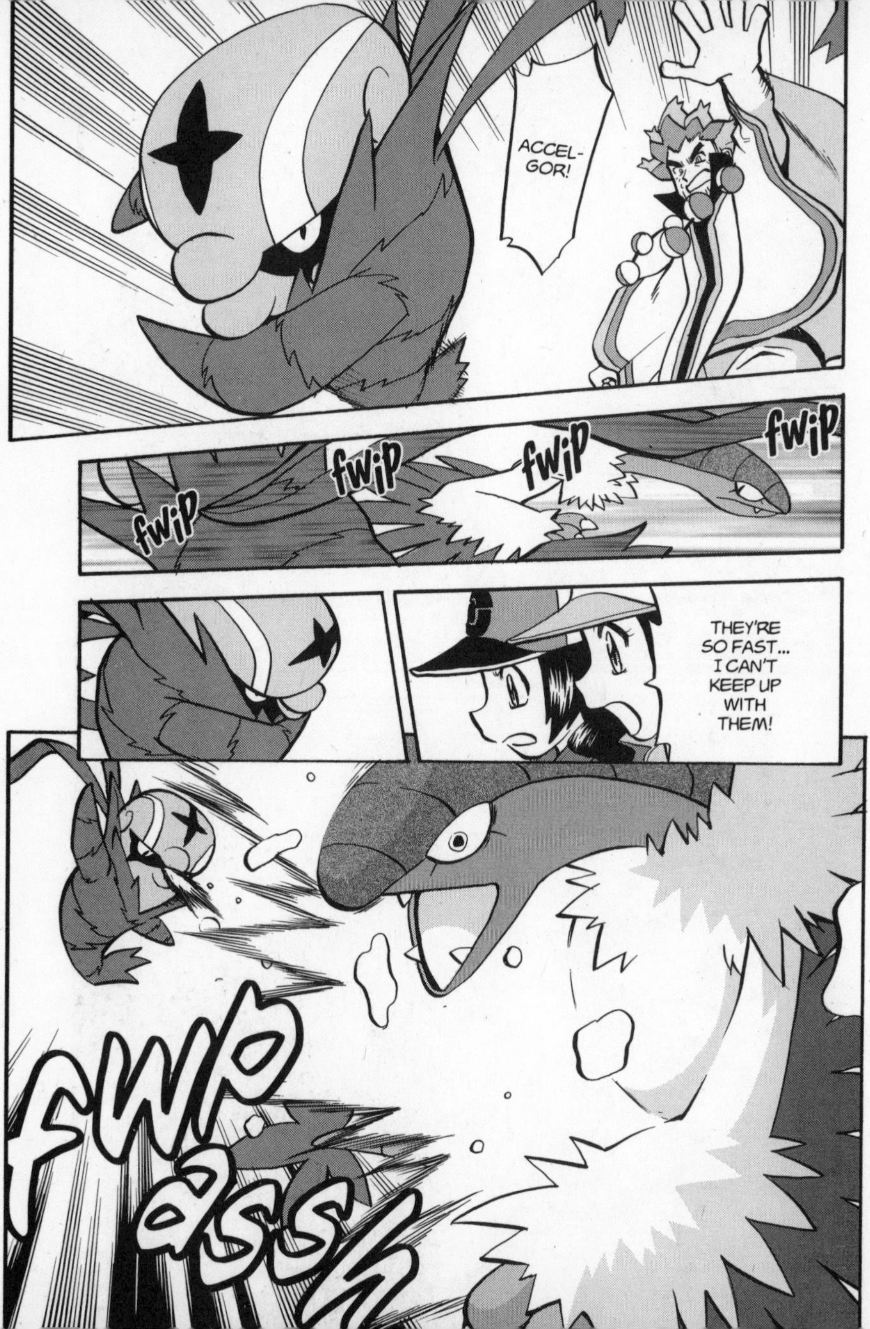
ACCEL-GOR!
fwip
fwip
fwip
fwip
THEY'RE SO FAST... I CAN'T KEEP UP WITH THEM!
fwp
assh

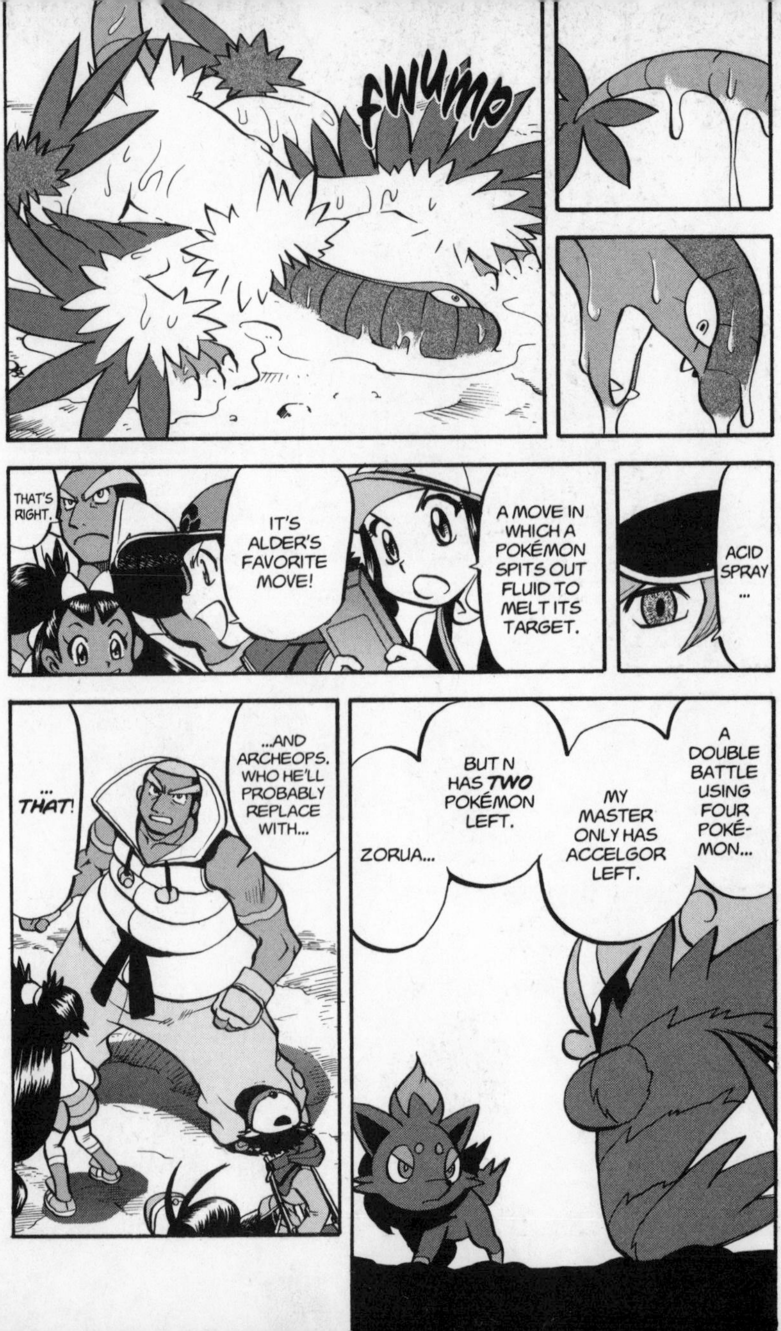
FWUMP
ACID SPRAY ...
A MOVE IN WHICH A POKÉMON SPITS OUT FLUID TO MELT ITS TARGET.
IT'S ALDER'S FAVORITE MOVE!
THAT'S RIGHT.
A DOUBLE BATTLE USING FOUR POKÉ-MON...
MY MASTER ONLY HAS ACCELGOR LEFT.
BUT N HAS TWO POKÉMON LEFT.
ZORUA...
...AND ARCHEOPS. WHO HE'LL PROBABLY REPLACE WITH...
... THAT!

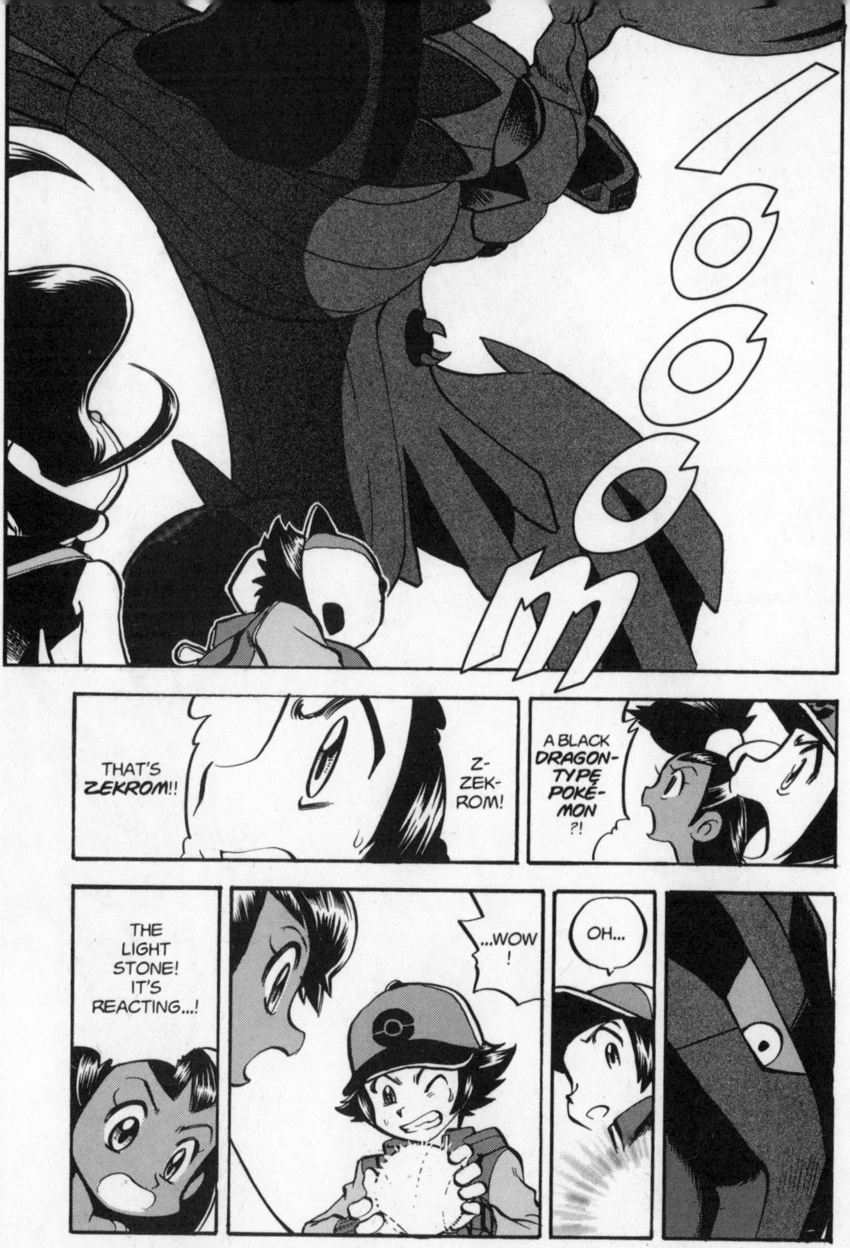
A BLACK DRAGON-TYPE POKÉMON?!
Z-ZEKROM!
THAT'S ZEKROM!!
OH...
...WOW!
THE LIGHT STONE! IT'S REACTING...!

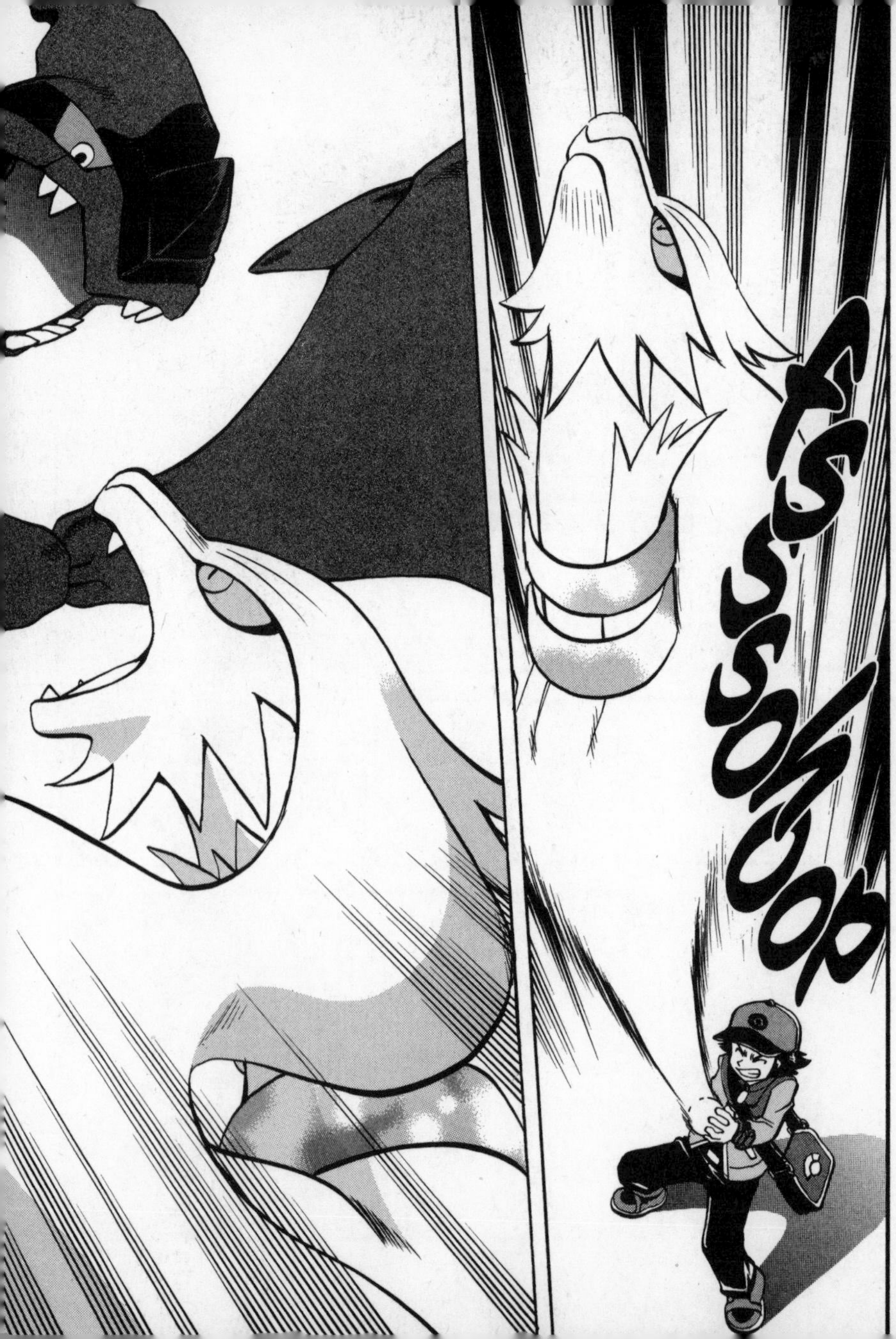
FSSSHOOOP

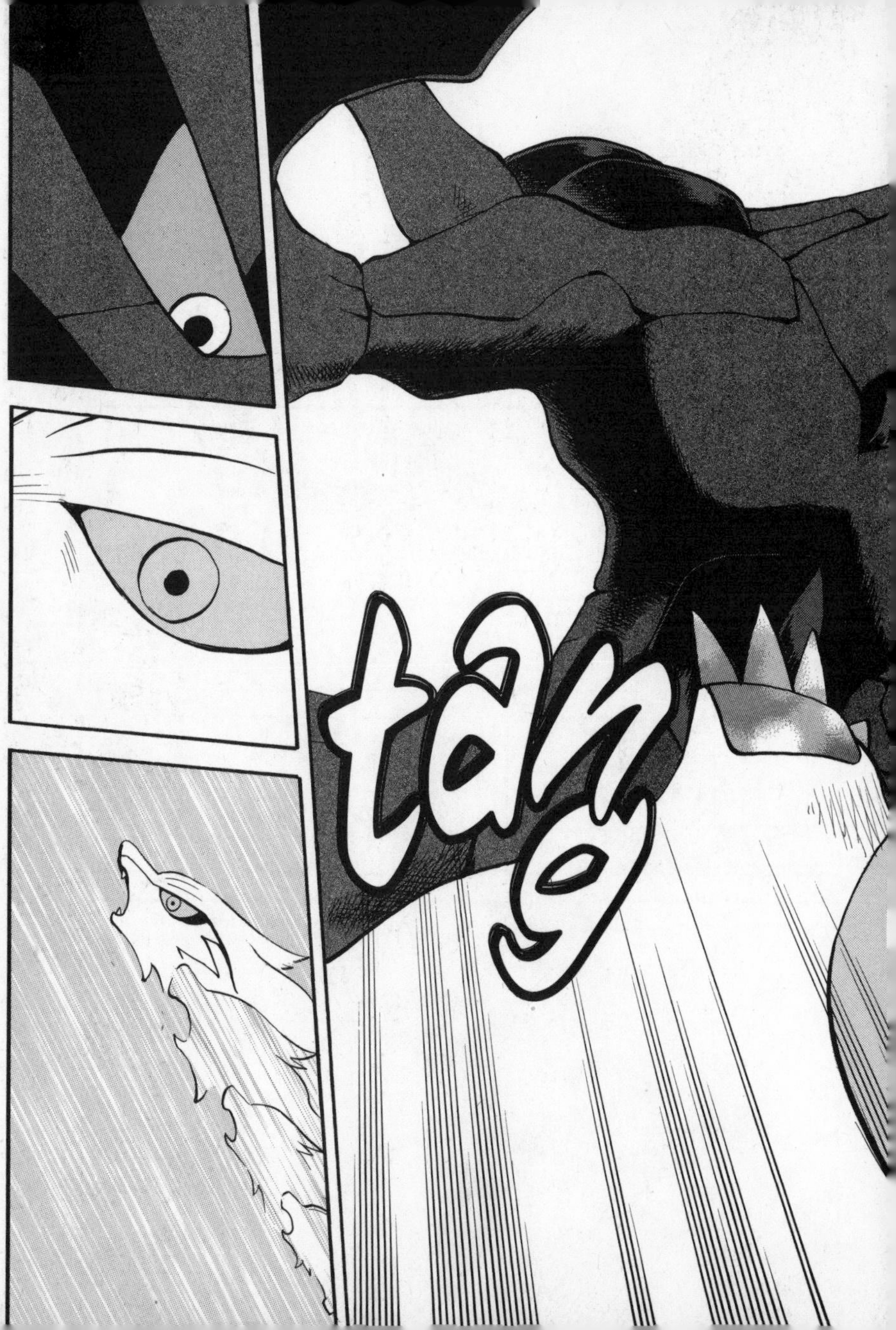
tang

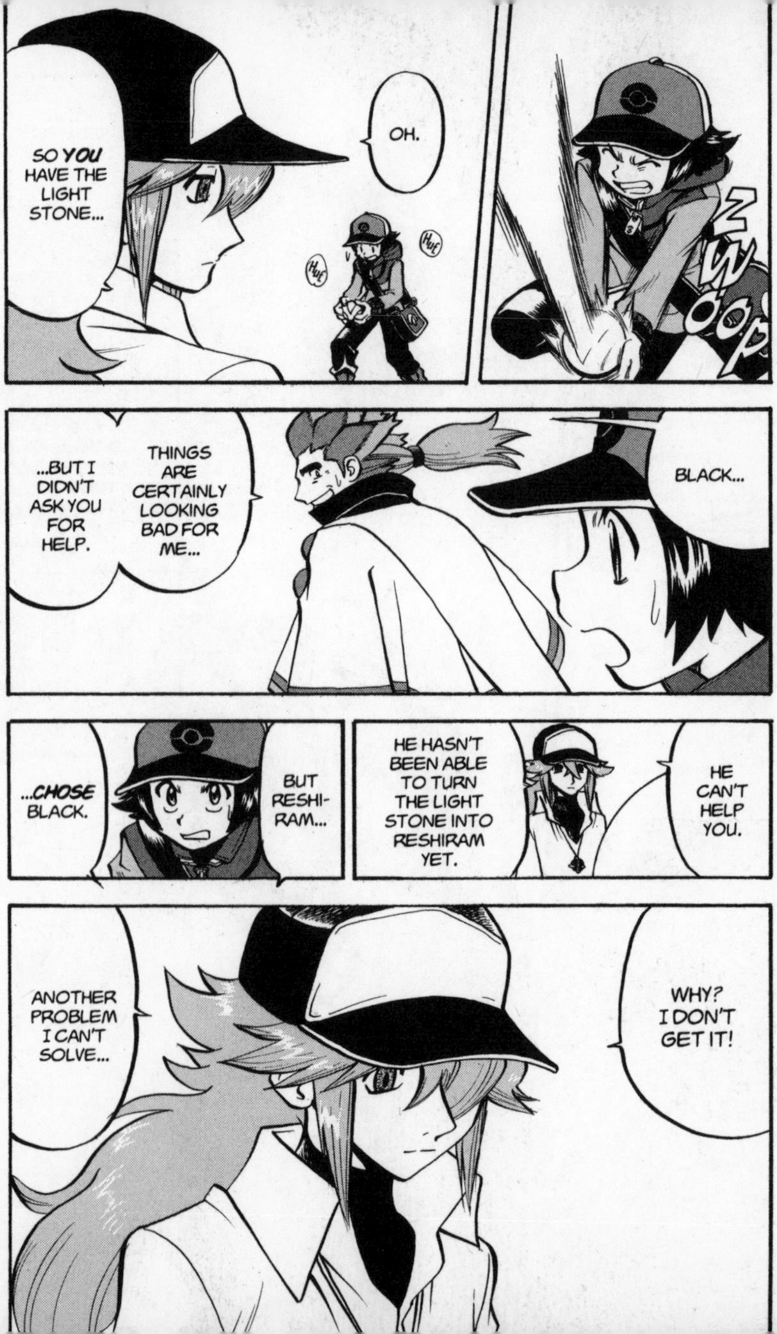
ZWOOP
OH.
Huf
Huf
SO YOU HAVE THE LIGHT STONE...
BLACK...
THINGS ARE CERTAINLY LOOKING BAD FOR ME...
...BUT I DIDN'T ASK YOU FOR HELP.
HE CAN'T HELP YOU.
HE HASN'T BEEN ABLE TO TURN THE LIGHT STONE INTO RESHIRAM YET.
BUT RESHI-RAM...
...CHOSE BLACK.
WHY? I DON'T GET IT!
ANOTHER PROBLEM I CAN'T SOLVE...

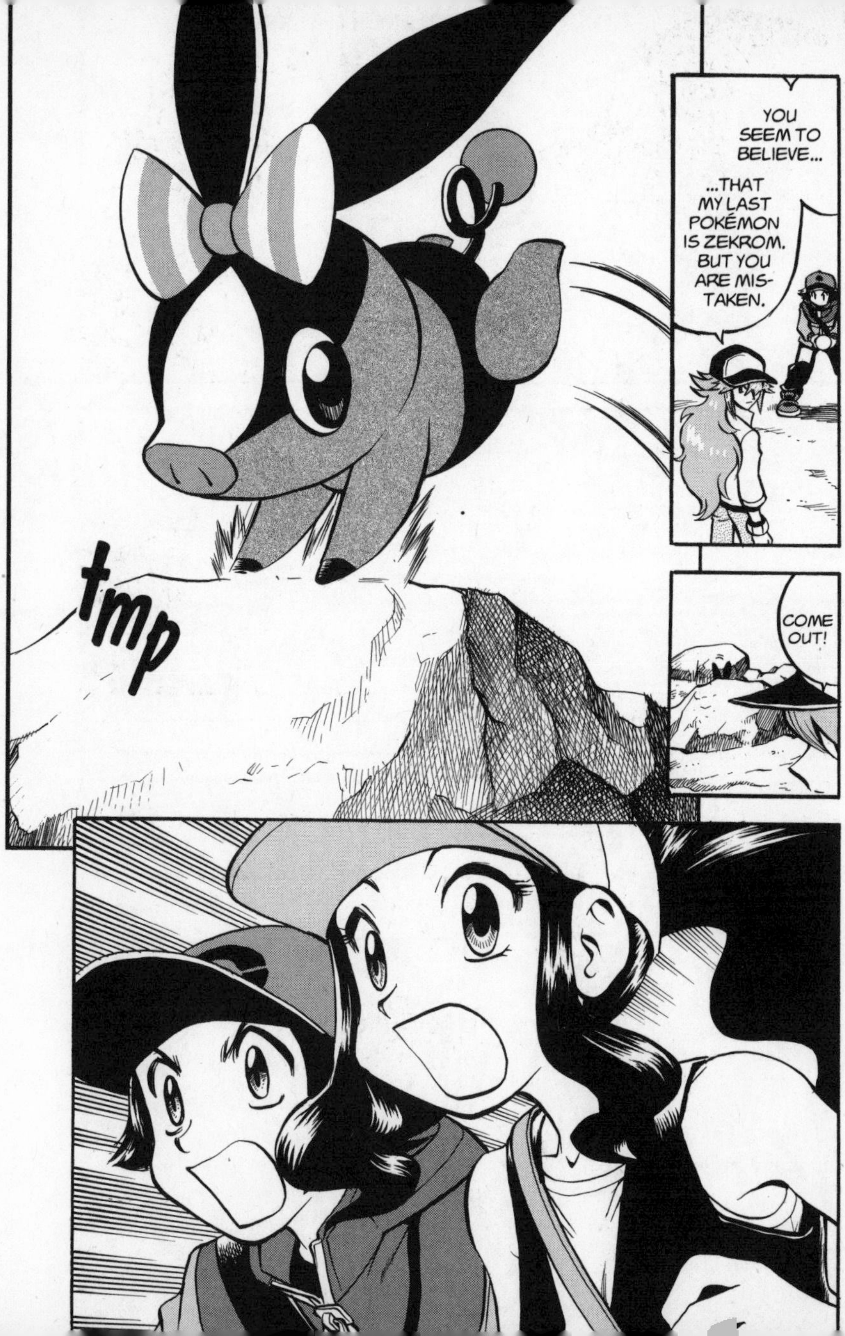
YOU SEEM TO BELIEVE...
...THAT MY LAST POKÉMON IS ZEKROM. BUT YOU ARE MIS-TAKEN.
COME OUT!
tmp

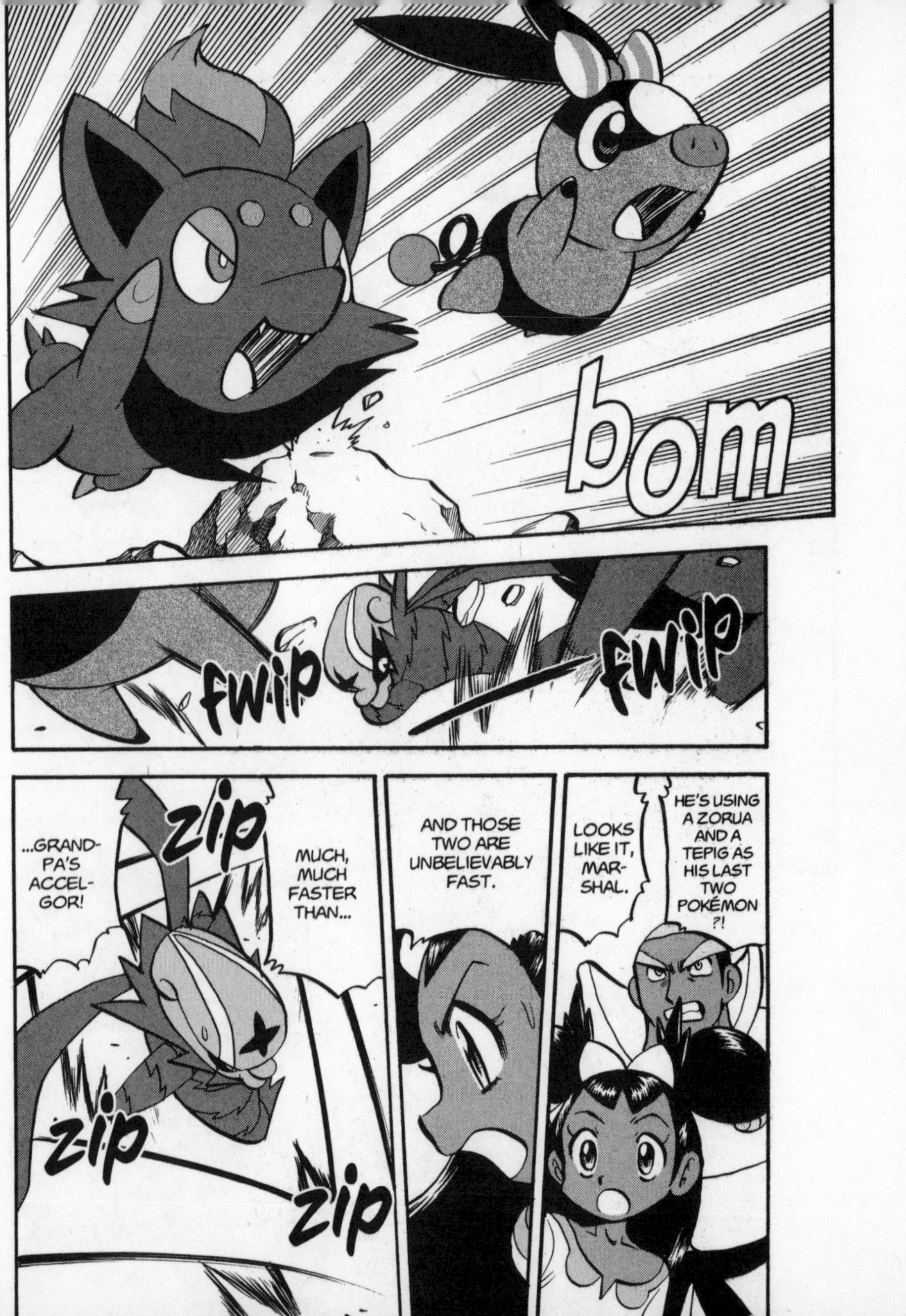
bom
fwip
fwip
HE'S USING A ZORUA AND A TEPIG AS HIS LAST TWO POKÉMON ?!
LOOKS LIKE IT, MAR-SHAL.
AND THOSE TWO ARE UNBELIEVABLY FAST.
MUCH, MUCH FASTER THAN...
...GRAND-PA'S ACCEL-GOR!
zip
zip
zip

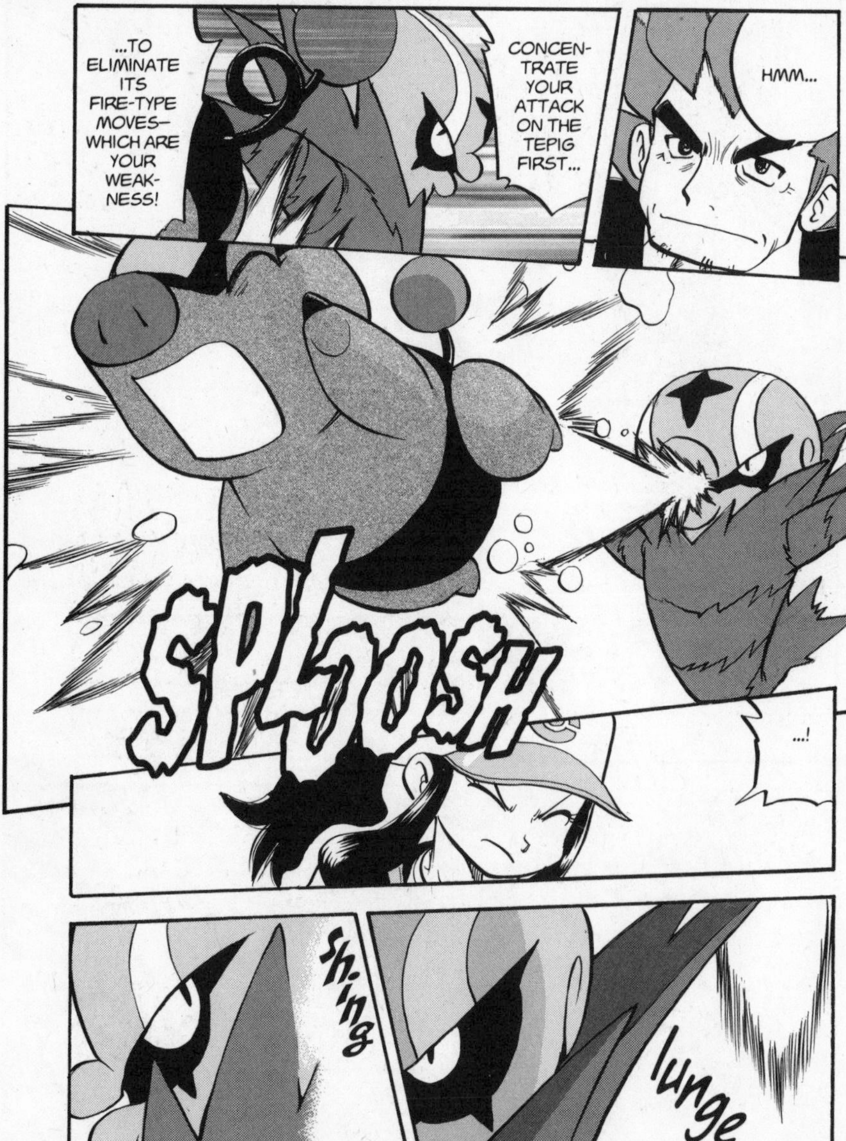
HMM...
CONCEN-TRATE YOUR ATTACK ON THE TEPIG FIRST...
...TO ELIMINATE ITS FIRE-TYPE MOVES—WHICH ARE YOUR WEAK-NESS!
SPLOOSH
...!
lunge
shing

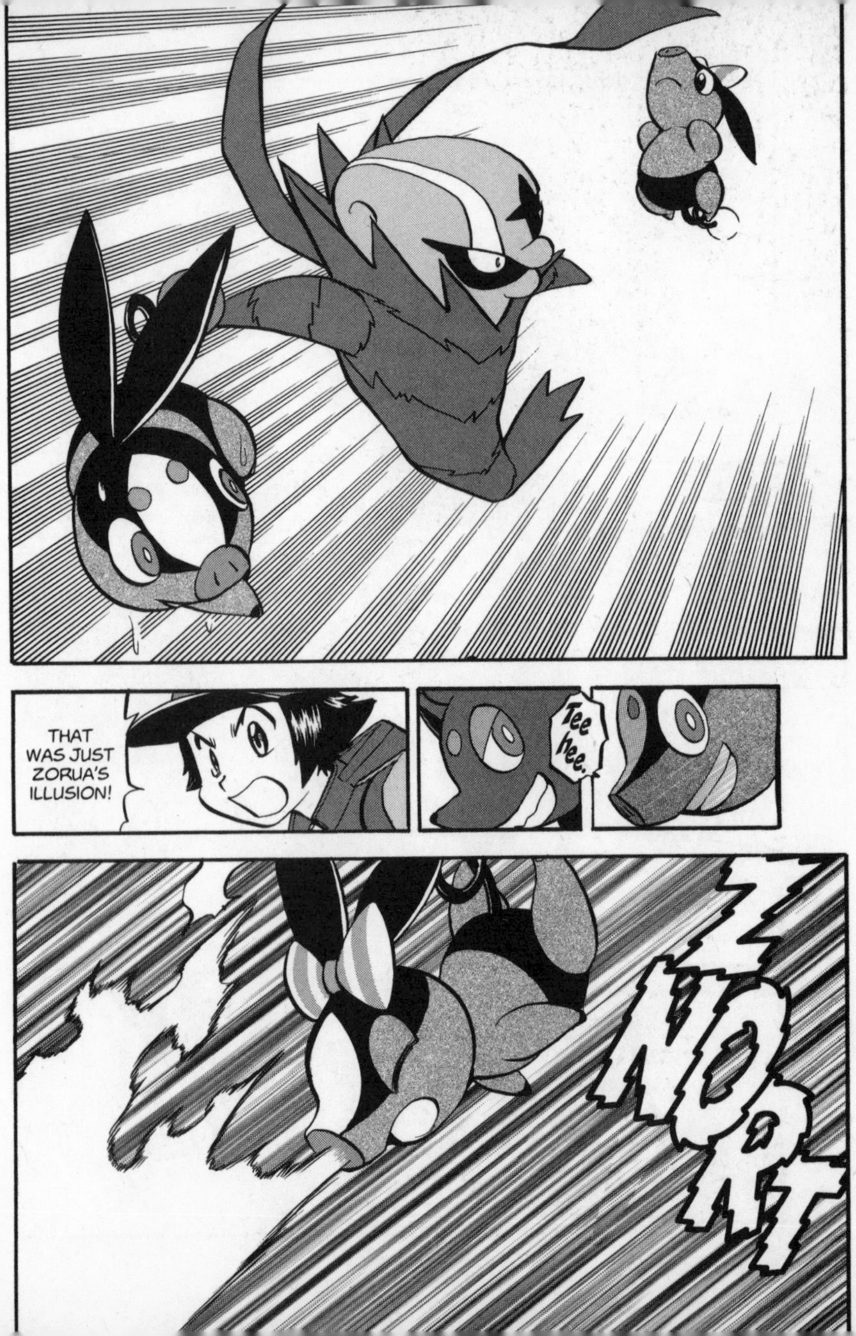
Tee hee.
THAT WAS JUST ZORUA'S ILLUSION!
SNORT

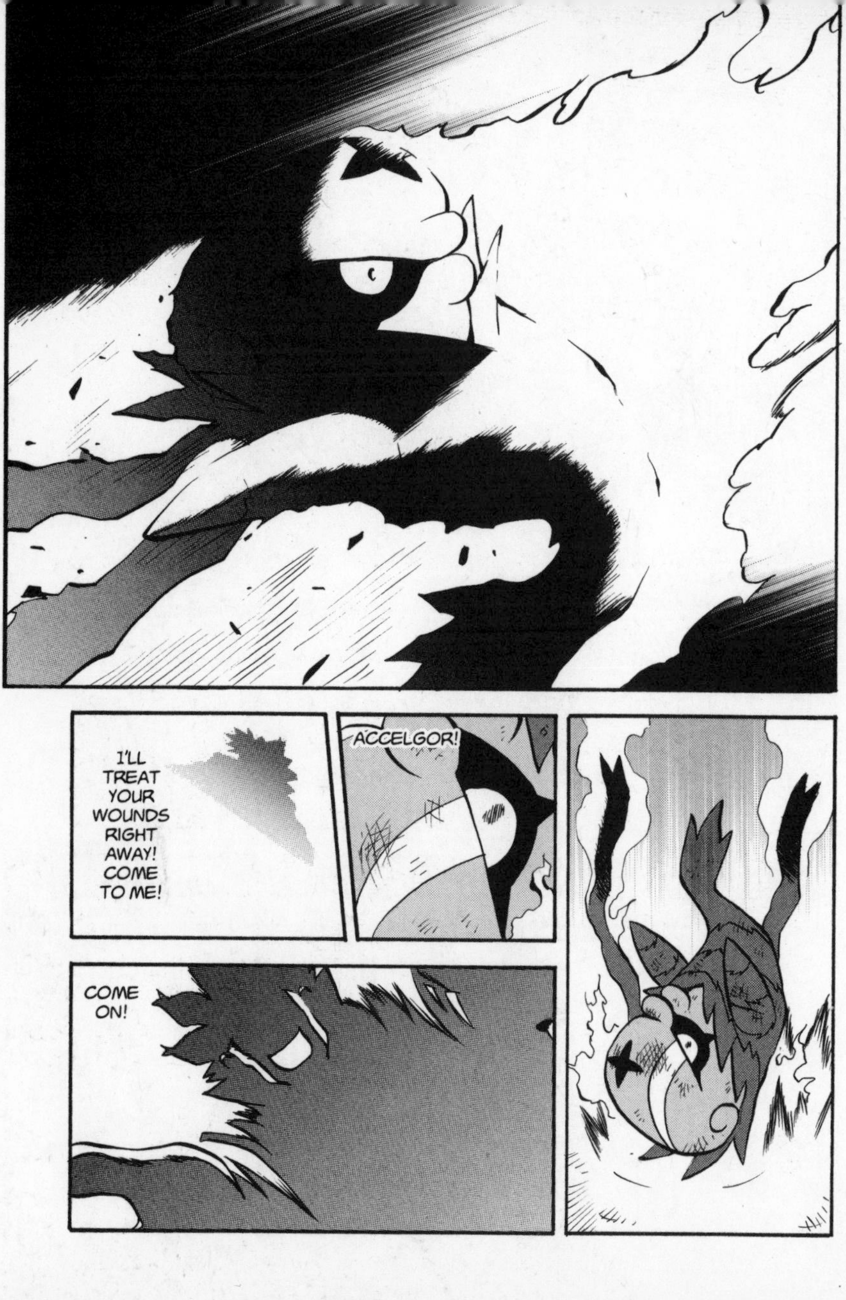
ACCELGOR!
I'LL TREAT YOUR WOUNDS RIGHT AWAY! COME TO ME!
COME ON!

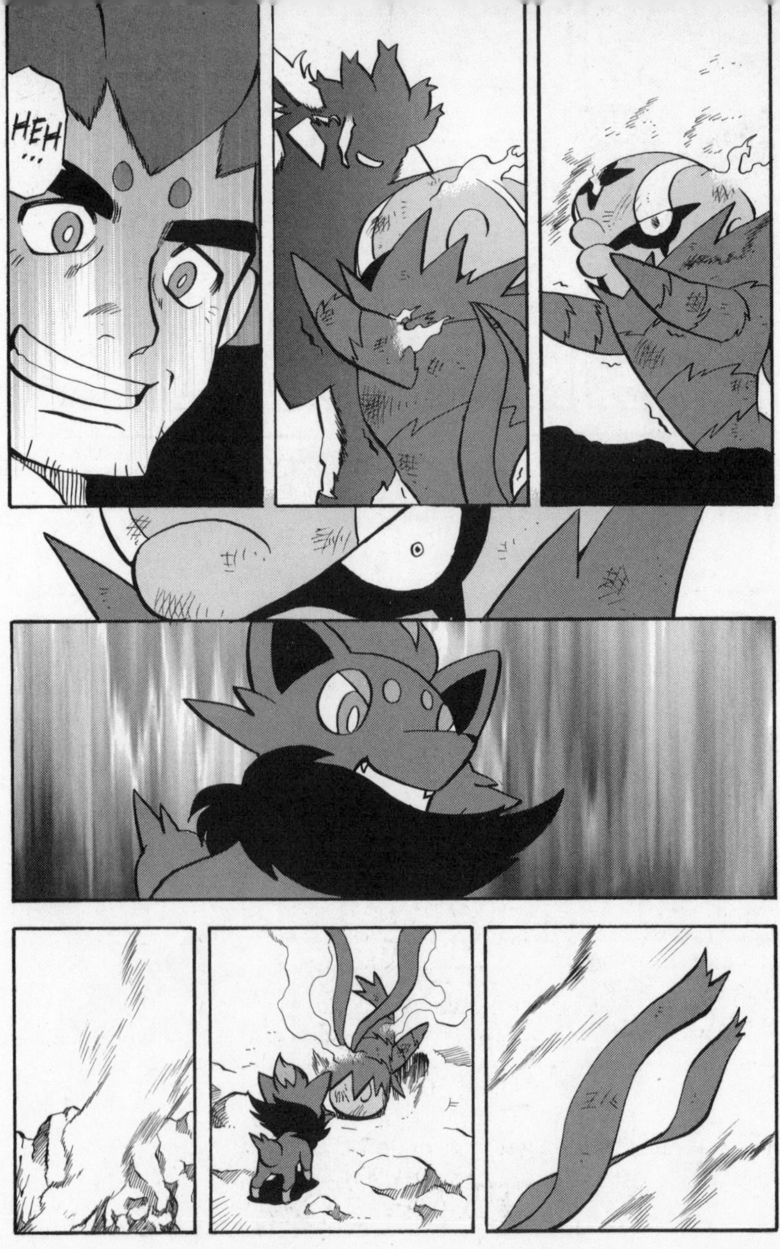
HEH ...

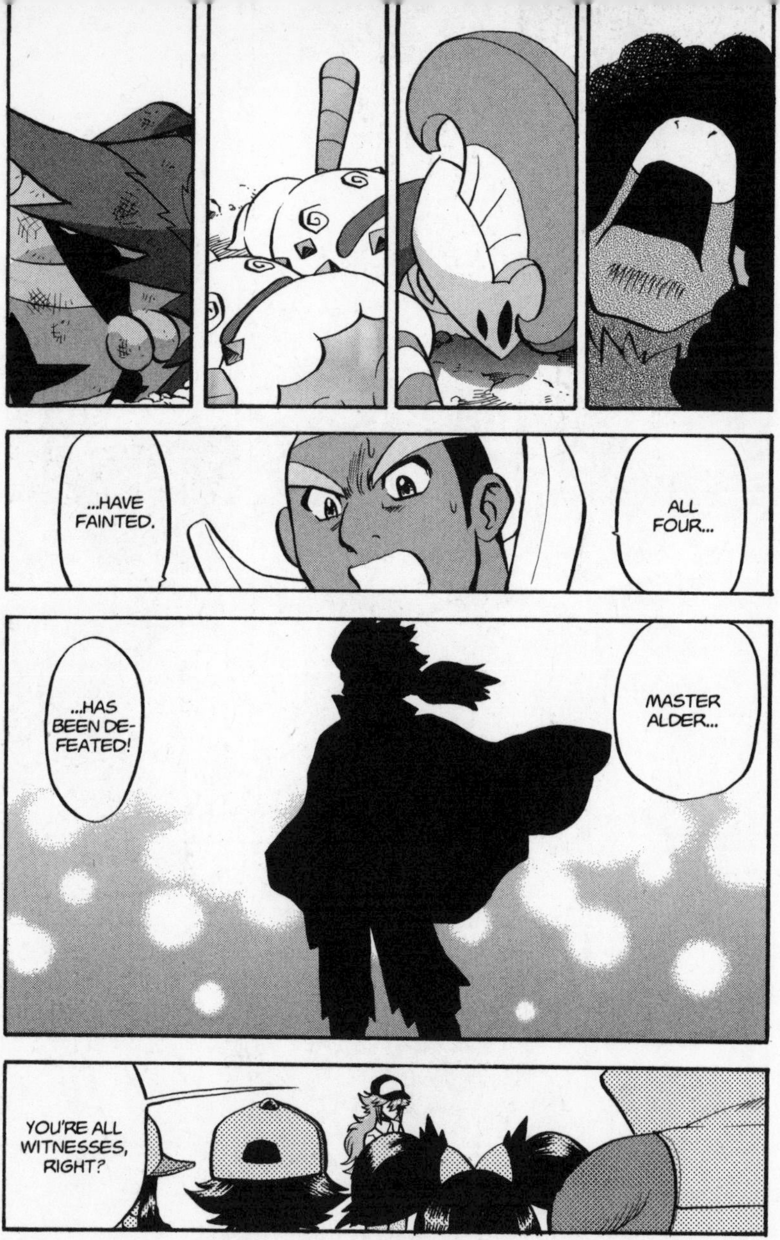
ALL FOUR...
...HAVE FAINTED.
MASTER ALDER...
...HAS BEEN DE-FEATED!
YOU'RE ALL WITNESSES, RIGHT?

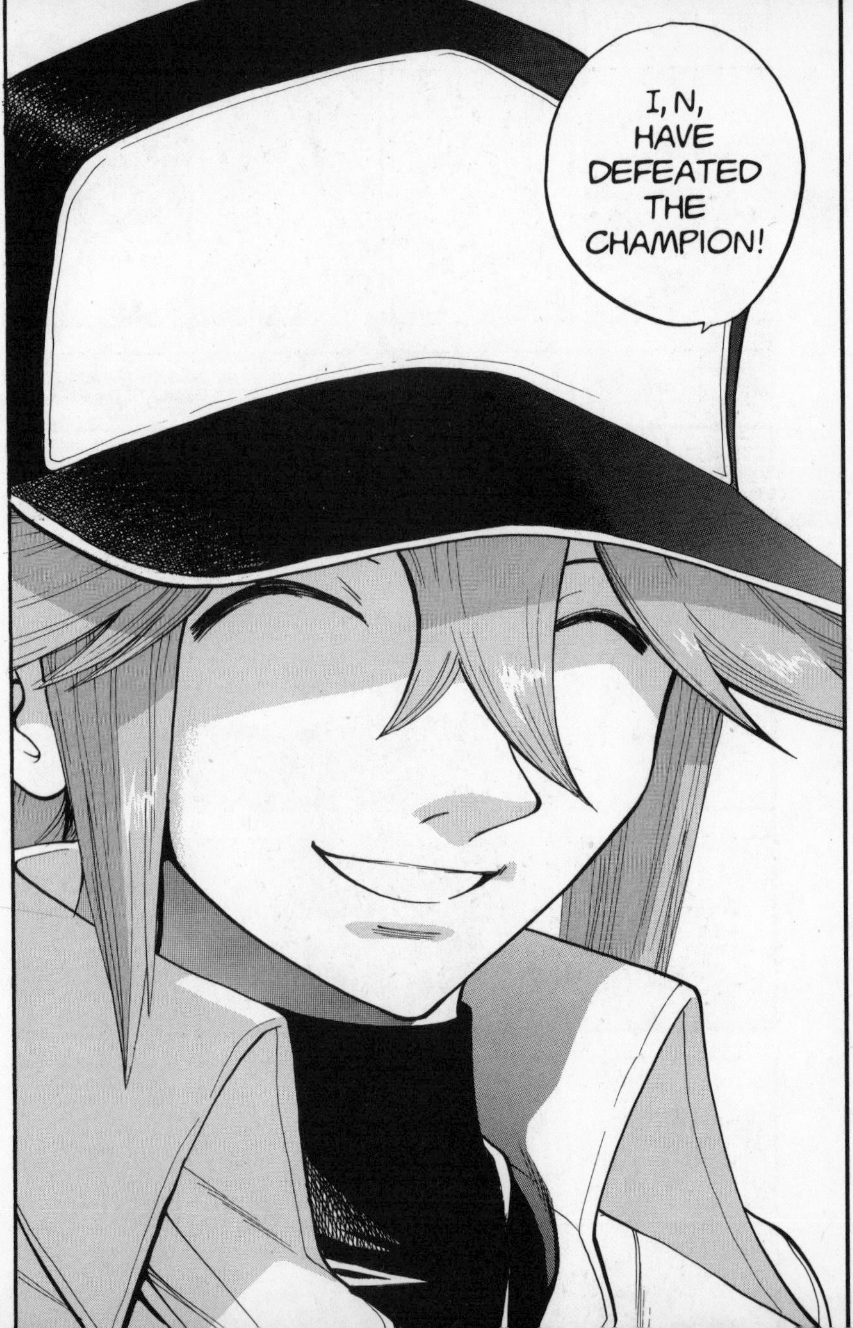
I, N, HAVE DEFEATED THE CHAMPION!

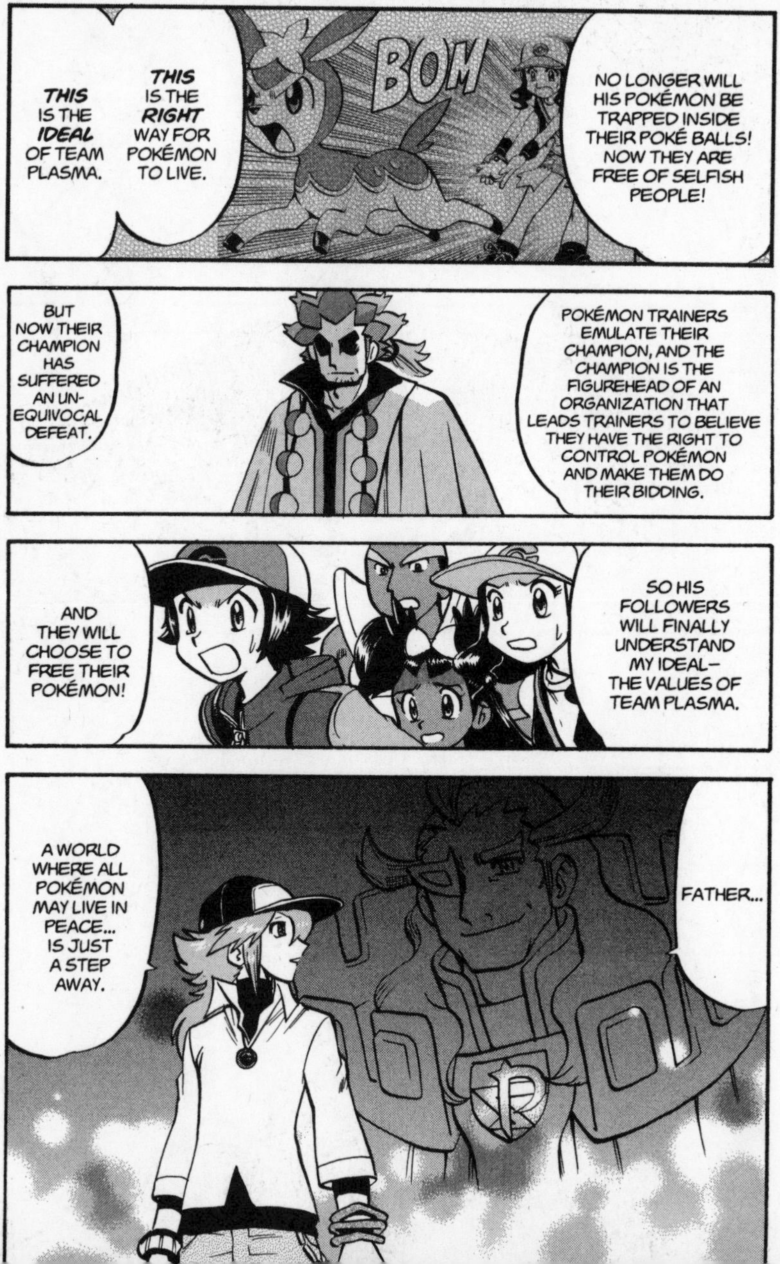
NO LONGER WILL HIS POKÉMON BE TRAPPED INSIDE THEIR POKÉ BALLS! NOW THEY ARE FREE OF SELFISH PEOPLE!
BOM
THIS IS THE RIGHT WAY FOR POKÉMON TO LIVE.
THIS IS THE IDEAL OF TEAM PLASMA.
POKÉMON TRAINERS EMULATE THEIR CHAMPION, AND THE CHAMPION IS THE FIGUREHEAD OF AN ORGANIZATION THAT LEADS TRAINERS TO BELIEVE THEY HAVE THE RIGHT TO CONTROL POKÉMON AND MAKE THEM DO THEIR BIDDING.
BUT NOW THEIR CHAMPION HAS SUFFERED AN UN-EQUIVOCAL DEFEAT.
SO HIS FOLLOWERS WILL FINALLY UNDERSTAND MY IDEAL— THE VALUES OF TEAM PLASMA.
AND THEY WILL CHOOSE TO FREE THEIR POKÉMON!
FATHER...
A WORLD WHERE ALL POKÉMON MAY LIVE IN PEACE... IS JUST A STEP AWAY.

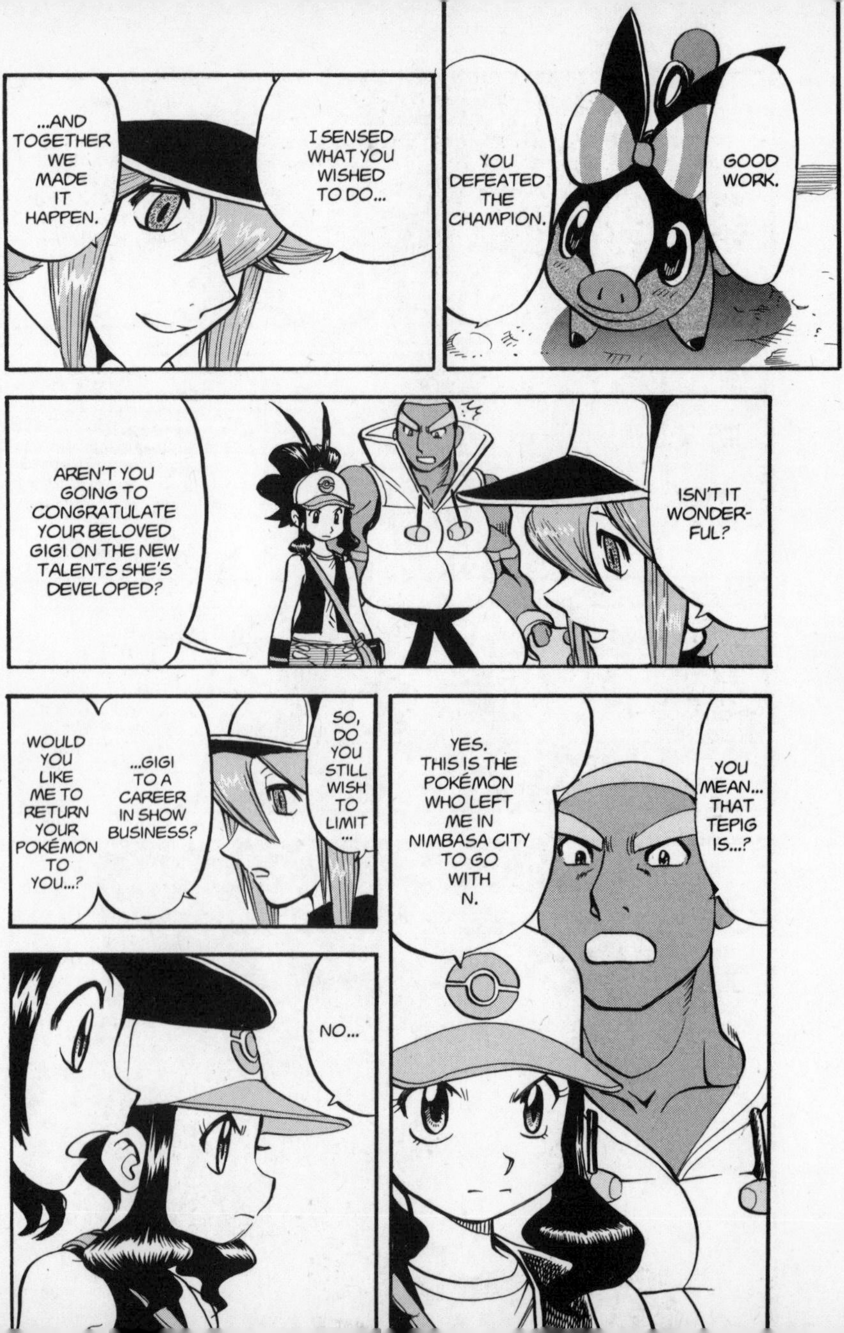
GOOD WORK.
YOU DEFEATED THE CHAMPION.
I SENSED WHAT YOU WISHED TO DO...
...AND TOGETHER WE MADE IT HAPPEN.
ISN'T IT WONDERFUL?
AREN'T YOU GOING TO CONGRATULATE YOUR BELOVED GIGI ON THE NEW TALENTS SHE'S DEVELOPED?
YOU MEAN... THAT TEPIG IS...?
YES. THIS IS THE POKÉMON WHO LEFT ME IN NIMBASA CITY TO GO WITH N.
SO, DO YOU STILL WISH TO LIMIT ...
...GIGI TO A CAREER IN SHOW BUSINESS?
WOULD YOU LIKE ME TO RETURN YOUR POKÉMON TO YOU...?
NO...

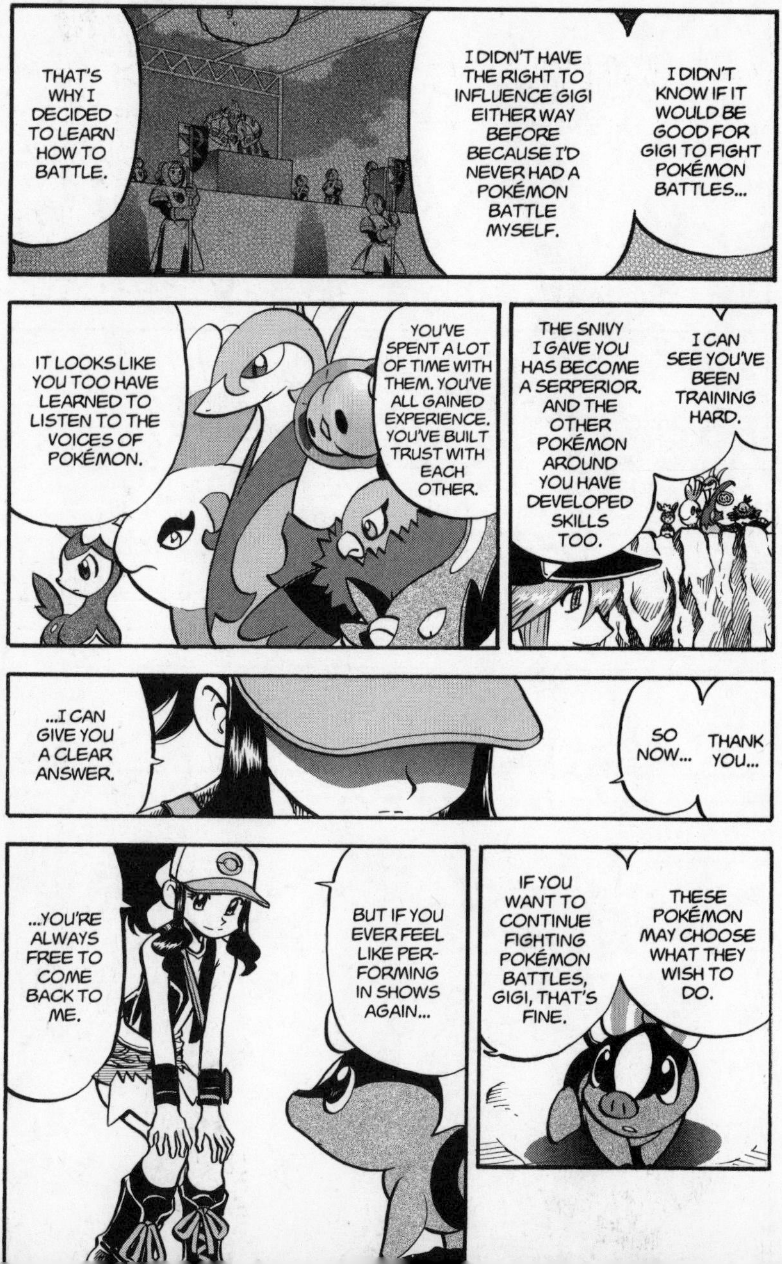
I DIDN'T KNOW IF IT WOULD BE GOOD FOR GIGI TO FIGHT POKÉMON BATTLES...
I DIDN'T HAVE THE RIGHT TO INFLUENCE GIGI EITHER WAY BEFORE BECAUSE I'D NEVER HAD A POKÉMON BATTLE MYSELF.
THAT'S WHY I DECIDED TO LEARN HOW TO BATTLE.
I CAN SEE YOU'VE BEEN TRAINING HARD.
THE SNIVY I GAVE YOU HAS BECOME A SERPERIOR. AND THE OTHER POKÉMON AROUND YOU HAVE DEVELOPED SKILLS TOO.
YOU'VE SPENT A LOT OF TIME WITH THEM. YOU'VE ALL GAINED EXPERIENCE. YOU'VE BUILT TRUST WITH EACH OTHER.
IT LOOKS LIKE YOU TOO HAVE LEARNED TO LISTEN TO THE VOICES OF POKÉMON.
THANK YOU...
SO NOW...
...I CAN GIVE YOU A CLEAR ANSWER.
THESE POKÉMON MAY CHOOSE WHAT THEY WISH TO DO.
IF YOU WANT TO CONTINUE FIGHTING POKÉMON BATTLES, GIGI, THAT'S FINE.
BUT IF YOU EVER FEEL LIKE PER-FORMING IN SHOWS AGAIN...
...YOU'RE ALWAYS FREE TO COME BACK TO ME.

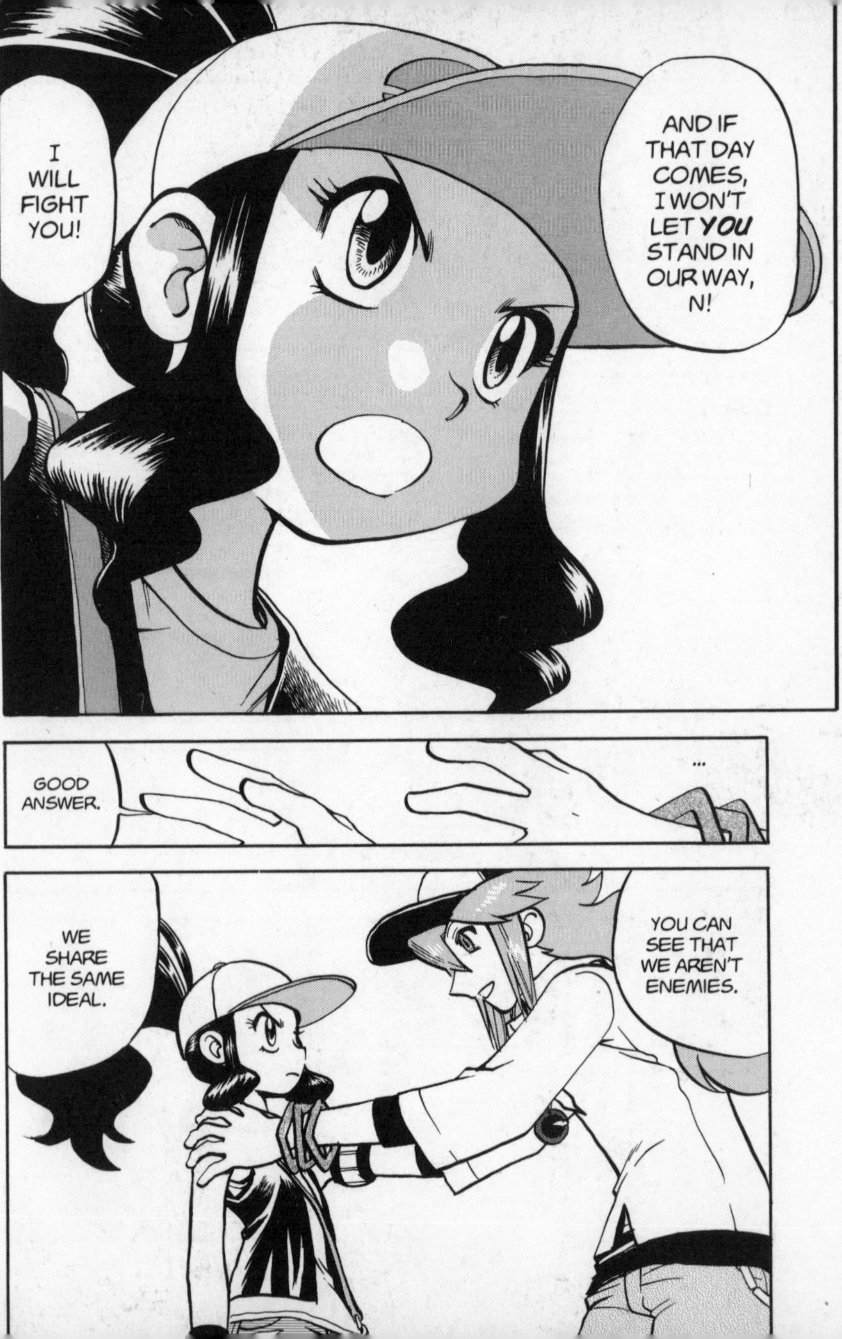
AND IF THAT DAY COMES, I WON'T LET **YOU** STAND IN OUR WAY, N!
I WILL FIGHT YOU!
...
GOOD ANSWER.
YOU CAN SEE THAT WE AREN'T ENEMIES.
WE SHARE THE SAME IDEAL.

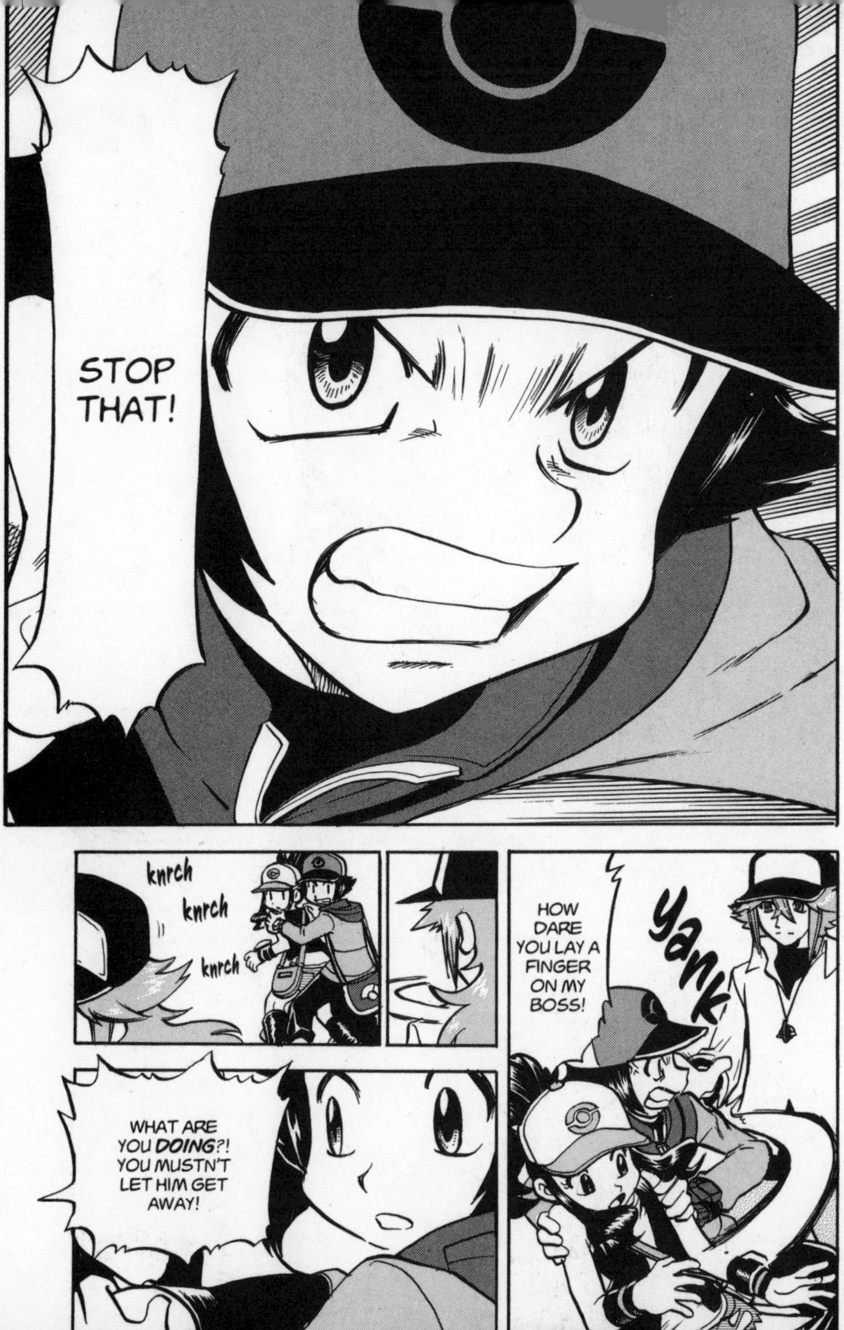
STOP THAT!
yank
HOW DARE YOU LAY A FINGER ON MY BOSS!
knrch
knrch
knrch
WHAT ARE YOU DOING?! YOU MUSTN'T LET HIM GET AWAY!

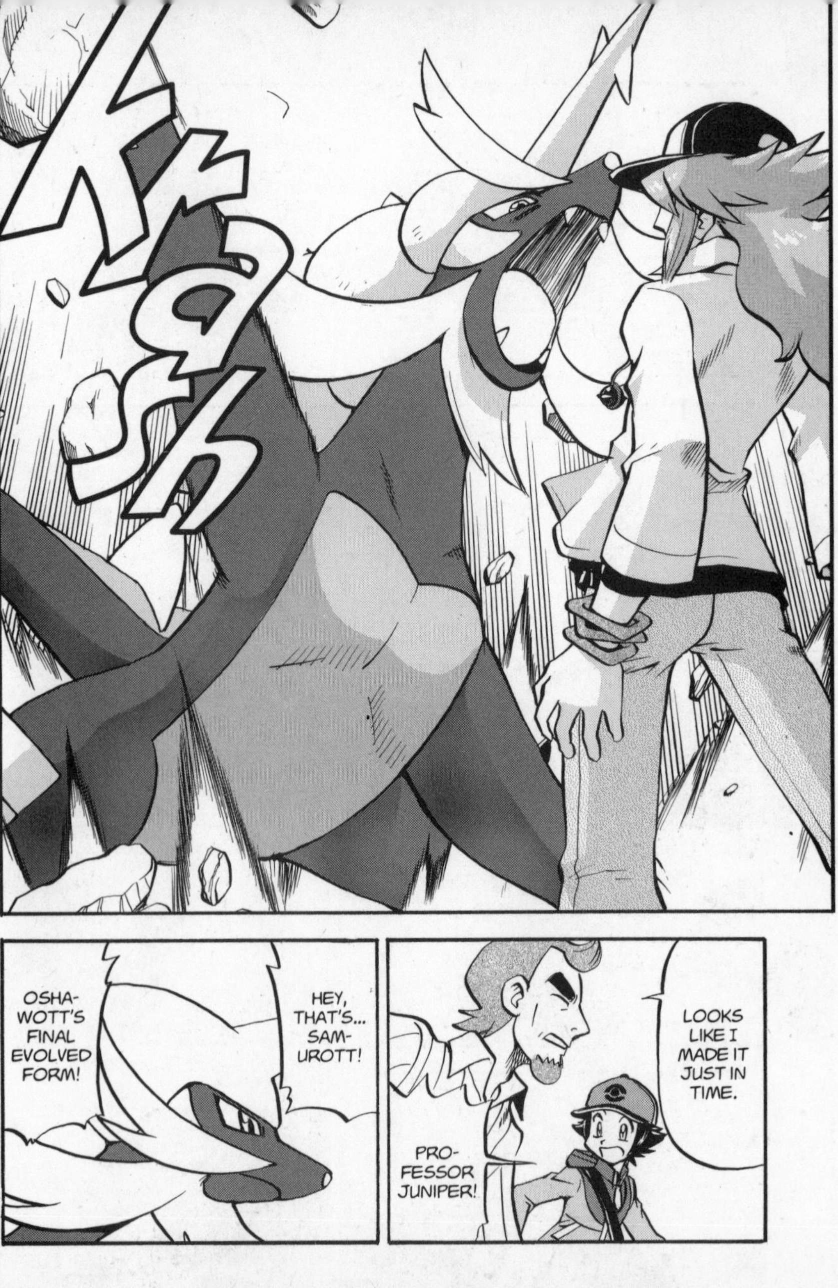
KRASH
LOOKS LIKE I MADE IT JUST IN TIME.
PRO-FESSOR JUNIPER!
HEY, THAT'S... SAM-UROTT!
OSHA-WOTT'S FINAL EVOLVED FORM!

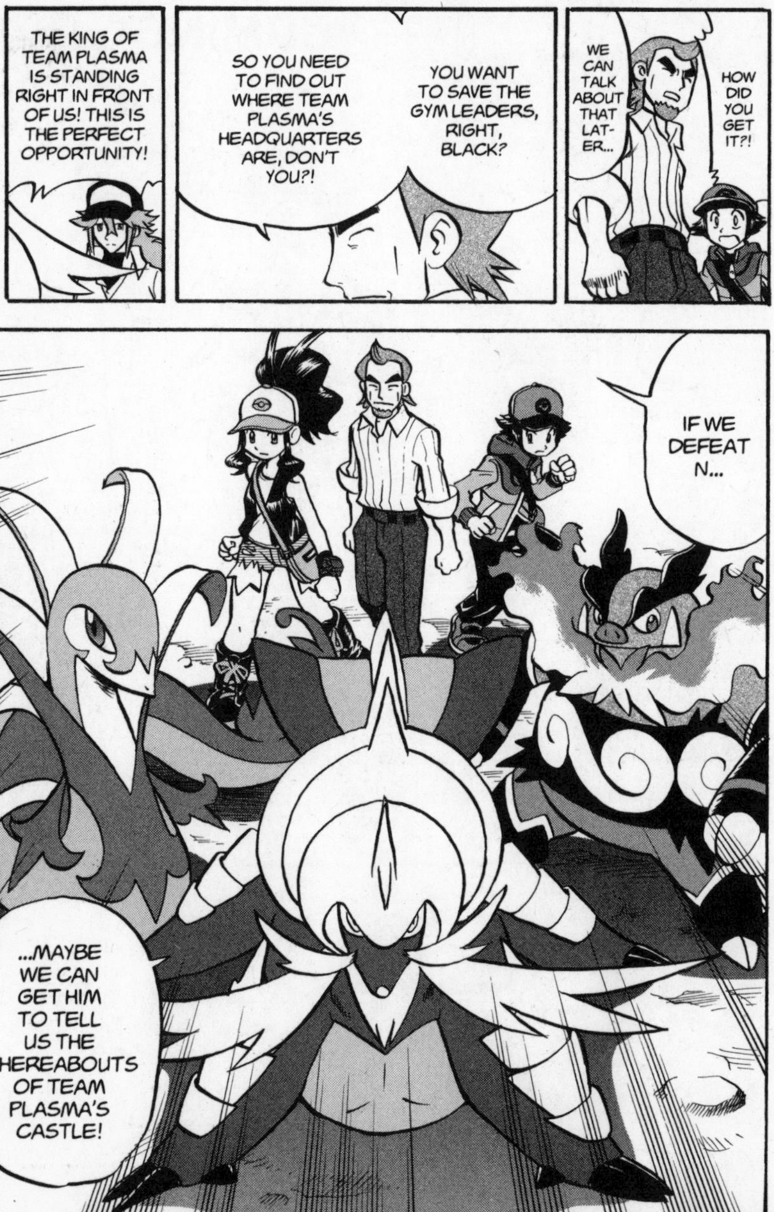
HOW DID YOU GET IT?!
WE CAN TALK ABOUT THAT LATER...
YOU WANT TO SAVE THE GYM LEADERS, RIGHT, BLACK?
SO YOU NEED TO FIND OUT WHERE TEAM PLASMA'S HEADQUARTERS ARE, DON'T YOU?!
THE KING OF TEAM PLASMA IS STANDING RIGHT IN FRONT OF US! THIS IS THE PERFECT OPPORTUNITY!
IF WE DEFEAT N...
...MAYBE WE CAN GET HIM TO TELL US THE WHEREABOUTS OF TEAM PLASMA'S CASTLE!

More Adventures COMING SOON...

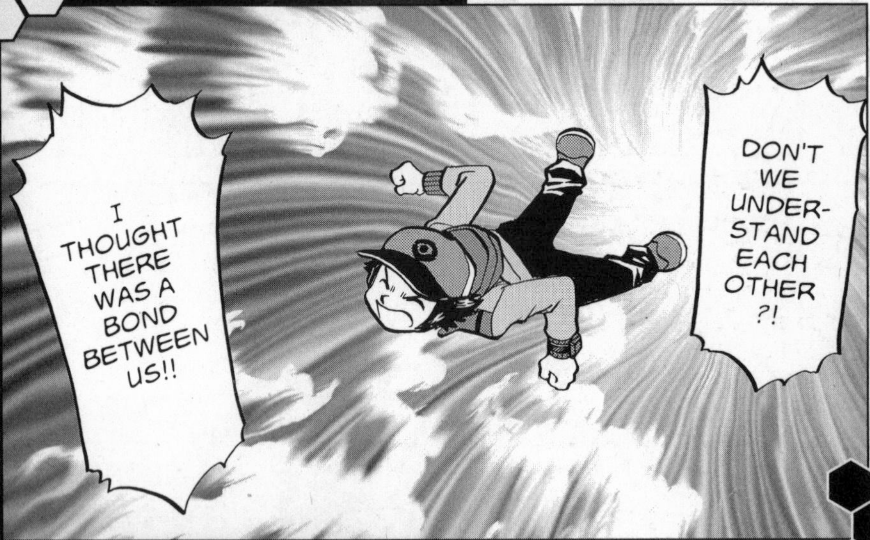
DON'T WE UNDER-STAND EACH OTHER ?!
I THOUGHT THERE WAS A BOND BETWEEN US!!

Team Plasma leader N shakes Black's faith in his relationship with his Pokémon. Then, just when Black is about to call it quits and go home, he gets a last-minute chance to earn the final Pokémon badge he needs to be eligible to compete in the Pokémon League!

HOW WILL BLACK REGAIN HIS CONFIDENCE IN TIME TO WIN THIS CRUCIAL GYM BATTLE...?

Plus, meet the Elite Four: Shauntal, Grimsley, Marshal and Caitlin!

VOL. 16 AVAILABLE NOW!

Start the adventures in Kalos with Pokémon X•Y, Vol. 1!

™

STORY BY
Hidenori Kusaka

ART BY
Satoshi Yamamoto

....

s the new champion of the Pokémon Battle Junior Tournament in the Kalos region, X is hailed as a child prodigy. But when the media ttention proves to be too much for him, he holes up in his room to hide from everyone—including his best friends. Then, his hometown f Vaniville Town is attacked by the two Legendary Pokémon Xerneas and Yveltal and a mysterious organization named Team Flare!

What will it take to get X to come out of hiding...?!
....

Only $4.99 US! ($5.99 in Canada)

Available at your local comic
book shop or bookstore!

ISBN: 978-1-4215-7980-1
Diamond Order Code: OCT141609

RATED
A
ALL AGES
ratings.viz.com

PERFECT SQUARE
www.PerfectSquare.com

VIZ
media
www.viz.com

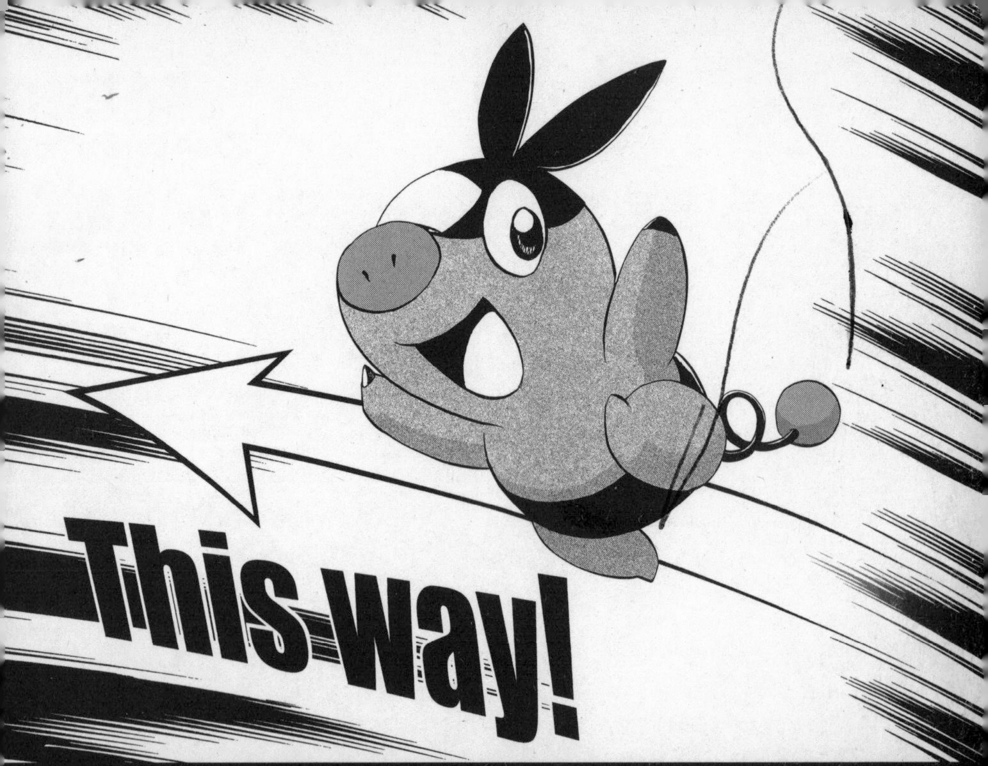
This way!

THIS IS THE END OF THIS GRAPHIC NOVEL!

To properly enjoy this VIZ Media graphic novel, please turn it around and begin reading from right to left.

This book has been printed in the original Japanese format in order to preserve the orientation of the original artwork. Have fun with it!

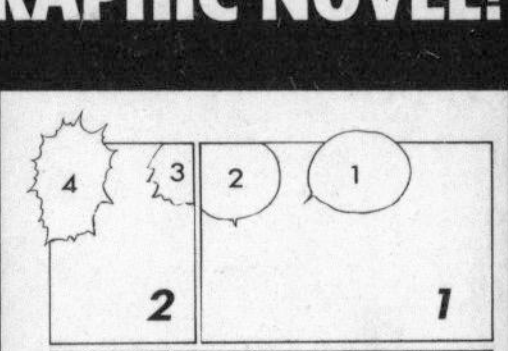
1
2
3
4
5
6
7
8
9
1
2
3
4
5

follow the action this way.